Shy Boy

The contract was still unsigned. He read it a final time, then initialled all the pages and signed the last one; he got his sister to witness it. He'd thought of asking Kerry, but maybe that was presuming too much.

There was still one final thing to do. The record didn't have a title yet, *The Girl With The Smile In Her Eyes* was only the working title – Tim Sloan thought it was a bit long to be the title when the record was released. Most records, he said, have only one or two words in the title, a maximum of three.

Jake had thought about it for a long time, and discussed his idea with Tony and Tim Sloan, both of whom liked it.

With trembling fingers, Jake filled in the blank space that had been left on the contract.

Kerry's Song, he wrote.

Also available in Point Romance

The Forget Me Not series:

Lavender Blue
Lorna Read

Silver Rose
Jill Eckersley

The White Cockade
Janis Dawson

The Wildest Dream
Kirsty White

Point Romance

Shy Boy

Kirsty White

SCHOLASTIC

Scholastic Children's Books
Commonwealth House, 1–19 New Oxford Street,
London WC1A 1NU, UK
A division of Scholastic Ltd
London ~ New York ~ Toronto ~ Sydney ~ Auckland

ISBN 0 590 19538 7

Typeset by TW Typesetting, Midsomer Norton, Somerset
Printed by Cox & Wyman Ltd, Reading, Berks.

10 9 8 7 6 5 4 3 2 1

Prologue

She saw him the first time she went to the mall, when she went with three girls she'd met at school. Kerry had only been in Alton for a matter of days; she was trying to get used to the bustle of the Surrey town after the quiet of the village in Cumbria where she'd grown up.

There had been a boy there, nothing serious, just an old friendship that had stretched into a date at a movie, then more dates at discos and parties. When Kerry left, she'd been relieved, in a way, because the relationship wasn't going anywhere.

I'll find someone else, she told herself.

She hadn't expected it to be so soon.

He was one of the buskers who played in the coffee bar at the mall; the blackboard told her that his name was Jake. He played the guitar and sang in a voice that sounded like brown velvet or double chocolate chip ice-cream.

As she talked to the girls she'd just met, Kerry

tried to ignore him, but she could not. She glanced at him constantly and, once or twice, she managed to gaze at him for a moment, as the others talked about somebody that she didn't know.

His face had strong features, a craggy jaw and a generous mouth. His hair was brown and just a little shaggy, as if it needed a good cut; she was just close enough to him to see that his eyes were a deep shade of blue. He looked as if he was older than her, but not by much.

Although it had been his voice that first attracted her to him, as she stared at him she realized that she liked the way he looked, too. There was a careless air about his appearance, as if he wasn't bothered about how he looked. Kerry liked that; she couldn't stand boys who were hung up on their looks.

When his spot ended, he put the guitar in its case and he walked away alone.

Then it was time to leave the mall; Kerry got up, pleased that the girls had asked her to come again. She'd been worried that she wouldn't make friends, but she liked all three of them.

On her way home, she kept on thinking about Jake. I'm sure I'll meet him soon, she thought. She couldn't wait for the chance to get to know him.

But Alton was different from the village where she'd grown up, where everybody had known everybody else. Corinne, Zoey and Julie never mentioned Jake and nor did anyone else. Kerry was too coy to ask about him; she didn't want anyone to know how she felt.

It was ridiculous, she thought, as her feelings grew stronger over the weeks and months that followed. She had a crush on him like a thirteen-year-old and she didn't even know his second name. She hadn't spoken to him and she didn't know when she would, if ever.

Spring became summer. In the holidays, Kerry got a temporary job on the local paper, the *Alton Gazette*. She was thrilled, because she wanted to be a reporter when she left school.

Every day, she met her friends for a coffee after work. She enjoyed their company but, most of all, she enjoyed Wednesdays and Fridays, when Jake played.

She'd almost given up hope of ever meeting him, but she continued to dream that she would.

1

Kerry walked along the street towards the mall. It was a beautiful day, she felt the slight breeze that was blowing through her hair.

Although she sometimes missed the village where she'd grown up, she liked Alton. The town centre was full of shops and cafés, and you could browse for hours in the mall.

She did not have a best friend yet. Because Zoey and Julie had steady boyfriends, Kerry spent most evenings and weekends with Corinne.

Corinne was Alton's golden girl, she was incredibly pretty, with long blonde hair; her father was a famous TV producer. Some of the girls at school didn't like Corinne, but Kerry put it down to jealousy: Corinne was friendly, and great fun to be with, she wasn't stuck-up or vain at all.

Corinne dated all the time, but never with the same boy more than once or twice. Kerry was the only one who never dated at all. She'd shrugged off her friends' efforts to find her a boyfriend, because the only boy she wanted to go out with was Jake. She couldn't help it, she was absolutely crazy about him; no one that she'd met came anywhere close.

She was careful to keep it a secret, feeling silly because she knew so little about him – only that his voice gave her goosebumps and when she thought about him she blushed automatically. When she was with the others, she resisted the urge to gaze at him, as she didn't want them to notice and guess about the way that she felt.

Often, she wondered if she should try to talk to him, but, if she did, she wouldn't know what to say. She consoled herself that she was bound to meet him sometime, but, as more and more time passed, even that possibility became more remote.

It was a lost cause, she thought, as she crossed the road to go into the mall.

A boy like that was bound to have a girlfriend, but she had watched carefully and had never seen any girl with him in the mall, and he always arrived and left alone.

Maybe there's hope, she thought, and then she said to herself, "in your dreams, Kerry".

As she walked into the mall, she heard the sound of him tuning his guitar and her heart lifted, as it always did.

Jake played the guitar for love. He had been playing for years, ever since his grandfather had given him a half-sized instrument for his eighth birthday. Now, at 18, he was going into his second year at college, studying music, and he had a proper guitar. He usually pretended that he was going to be a teacher, but in his dreams he had a recording contract and wrote songs that people loved to hear.

He strummed a chord to check the tuning, smiling to himself as he adjusted the high E string. He had five brothers and sisters and, with three of them being students, it was a struggle to make ends meet – he had to work to make up the shortfall in his grant. During the summer, he worked in the Post Office sorting office from six in the morning until two in the afternoon and then, later, he delivered leaflets around the town for a couple of pounds per hundred. In the evenings, he washed dishes in a restaurant. Twice a week, he played at the shopping mall; he didn't get paid anything for it beyond what people dropped in the collection box, but the chance to play to an audience was important to him.

At college, Jake had made a demo tape of some of his songs and sent it off to a record company. Although he had sent the tape with return postage, he had heard nothing for a month. In a way, he did not expect to, because the record companies got hundreds of tapes every week and they only took on a couple of new artistes every year. In the basement of his house, he had built a makeshift practice studio with a couple of microphones and an old Teac reel-to-reel tape recorder. He was saving hard because he wanted to buy a new electric guitar, but he doubted if he'd be able to afford one this year.

He turned on the amplifier, wincing at the brief

whine of feedback. He began to play, first of all his own arrangement of *Love is All Around* and then a song he had written himself. People drinking coffee stopped talking and listened; Jake was really good at what he did.

When he paused between numbers, he looked around, then he saw her sitting there with her friends. Jake had heard one of the other girls call her Kerry; he reckoned that she was a couple of years younger than him. He really liked her; he wanted to get to know her, but he didn't know how.

He'd often seen her in the mall, he liked to think that maybe she enjoyed listening to him, but she was always talking to her friends. He'd never had the chance to speak to her, and even if he did, what would he say? He had little free time and no money. And, apart from anything else, although he could play to an audience, Jake was shy when he was on his own with a girl that he liked.

He remembered a tip about performing he had read in music magazine: don't play to the entire audience, play just to one person.

When he began to sing next, he was singing to Kerry.

Kerry gazed at Jake, her cappuccino forgotten. He sounded so good and he looked so nice; she'd give anything to be able to talk to him, to get to know him better. But it was an impossible dream, the kind of thing that happens in fairy-tales, not real life.

Zoey finished the story she was telling; Julie

and Corinne laughed in response. Kerry, who hadn't been listening, blushed deeply; she'd been lost in her thoughts and had been staring at Jake for far too long.

"Are you coming?" Corinne asked her.

"What?" Kerry had no idea what she was talking about.

Corinne sighed. "Nick's party. On Saturday. His parents have promised to stay out of the way. It should be great."

"I suppose," Kerry said, cupping her head in her hands, consciously avoiding looking at Jake.

"I think she fancies him," Julie said.

"Who, Nick?" Corinne asked.

"No," Julie said. "That bloke who plays the guitar. She's been staring at him for ages."

Kerry flushed deep crimson. The others laughed.

Zoey glanced at Jake. "Jake Michaels, he's called. My brother knows him. He's at college, doing music. He's supposed to be really good."

"Why didn't you tell me before?" Kerry blurted, without thinking.

Zoey shrugged. "You never asked."

"You *do* fancy him," Julie said.

Kerry looked down at her cooling cappuccino, deeply embarrassed that her secret was out.

"He *is* good," Zoey said. "Chris says he plays at the college dances. He might make it, you know. I mean, he might be a rock star."

"And then he might just end up as just another homeless busker," Corinne sniffed. She opened her bag and took out her purse. "Anyone for another coffee?"

Kerry shook her head; Corinne's remark had annoyed her. The skin of her face was still burning. She wished that she had wings and could just fly away, out of the mall, far from her friends. Zoey reached over and touched her hand briefly.

"It was bound to come out sometime," she said.

Kerry shook her head. She didn't want it to come out at all.

Corinne came back with a tray of coffees. She waved away the money Julie and Zoey offered. Corinne's father gave her plenty of money; she was the only one of the girls who didn't have a summer job. Julie and Zoey were stacking shelves at the supermarket; Kerry was lucky to have her job on the *Alton Gazette*, even though she was just a lowly news desk assistant. She'd been given the job after a story she'd written had won a prize in a competition, but she didn't actually write anything, all she did was make endless cups of tea.

Corinne shook her long blonde hair and smiled at Kerry. "I bet you've never even talked to him."

Jake was doing a Simon and Garfunkel song; Kerry had seen a woman go up to him, she supposed he'd been asked to sing it. Her parents had the album it came from; she sometimes played it herself.

When Jake finished the song, Corinne stood up and grabbed Kerry's hand.

"Come on," she said, marching towards Jake and dragging Kerry with her.

Kerry was so taken aback that, at first, she didn't resist. When she came to her senses, it was too late, she was within a few steps of Jake and Corinne was brightly opening her mouth to say "hello". Kerry gulped and looked down, hoping that the floor would open and swallow her up.

"Hi," Corinne said.

"Hello," Jake replied.

Kerry looked up then. For a moment her eyes met Jake's and his were open and kind; there was a light in them as if he was pleased to see her. Her stomach lurched and she opened her mouth to say something, but it was already too late, Corinne was barging on.

"There's a party on Saturday night," she was saying, "I was wondering if you'd like to come along? You could sing some songs, if you like."

Jake's eyes held Kerry's for a moment longer, then his attention shifted to Corinne.

"I can't," he said, "I'm busy."

His words struck Kerry like a blow, she felt pain as if she'd been slapped. All at once she was thinking, he doesn't like me, I've upset him, of course he's busy on Saturday because someone like him has a girlfriend. Of course.

"What a pity," Corinne said. "Some other time, maybe?"

"Maybe," Jake said. "But I'm kind of busy most of the time."

Somehow, Kerry got back to her seat. She sat down, blinking back the tears that had sprung to her eyes. Zoey was looking at her quizzically, Corinne just acted as if nothing had gone on.

"What happened?" Julie asked.

"I just asked him to Nick's party, but he can't

make it," Corinne said. "You know, nothing ventured, nothing gained."

Kerry just sat there, thinking of the broken pieces of her dream lying on the ground like shattered glass. She felt the blood drain from her face. It was over now, she thought, the end of all her hopes.

Corinne sighed. "I just wanted to play matchmaker, that's all."

"Maybe you should've asked Kerry first," Zoey said carefully.

Corinne shrugged. "I knew she'd say no."

Zoey shook her head. Kerry looked at Corinne, and knew that she'd never forgive her for making a fool of her like that.

On Saturday, Kerry lay on her bed, staring at the ceiling. She'd spent the whole day doing that. Friday night as well. As far as the world was concerned, she was reading a book; she just couldn't bear it if anyone found out how she felt.

The hurt she felt was a physical pain that was lodged deep in her stomach like undigested stodge. She kept on thinking back to the day before, to the moment when she'd been so happy just watching Jake and dreaming about him. She'd played out the scene so many times in her mind, the first moment she met him, actually to speak to. It went something like this:

They were alone, just the two of them, maybe in the coffee bar on a very quiet day. He was looking at her and she was looking at him; they just smiled for ages and ages.

And then he said, "You know, I used to look at you all the time when I was playing in the mall. I used to wonder when I'd ever get to meet you."

Then she'd giggle, and say, "I used to look at you too."

Her dream hadn't gone on beyond that, but at least it had reached that moment when she felt the joy of knowing that he cared about her too.

Now it was all over, she couldn't even dream any more.

She'd been over the whole thing endless times in her head, she'd even written it all down and then torn up the paper into little shreds because it was so silly. It was all over, Jake wasn't interested, there was nothing else she could do.

Except give up.

The only thing that niggled at her was the way he'd looked at her when their eyes first met; she hadn't detected disdain or disinterest, if anything, she'd felt the opposite. From a tiny moment, she thought, even knew instinctively, that he liked her too.

But then he said that he was busy, and when Corinne had asked again, he said he was kind of busy most of the time. If he had liked her at all, he wouldn't've said that, he would've left the way open somehow for them to meet again.

The doorbell rang. Kerry shifted and sighed, and wondered if the excuse about the book would last for the whole weekend, then she heard Corinne's voice and her footsteps coming up the stairs.

She swore underneath her breath. She didn't want to see Corinne, but she hadn't said anything because she didn't want her parents to wonder why.

Dully, she opened the door and let Corinne in.

She sat down on the bed, tossing her hair over her shoulder. She was wearing a new dress that Kerry had seen in the most expensive shop in the mall, and she looked fantastic. When she saw that Kerry was wearing shorts and a T-shirt, she frowned.

"You haven't forgotten," she said.

"Forgotten what?"

"Nick's party. You *have* to come."

Kerry blinked. "I … I haven't got anything to wear," she said, lamely.

Corinne shook her head. "You've got that dress, you know, the one with that crazy print."

Kerry shook her head. "It's in the wash."

"Well, you've got that yellow one, or that denim skirt with the top…"

Kerry shook her head vigorously.

"If all else fails, you've got these new jeans and that silky top."

Kerry frowned.

"Is there something wrong?" Corinne asked her.

Kerry looked up at the ceiling.

"There *is* something wrong," Corinne said.

Kerry stood up and stared out of the window. "I just wish you hadn't dragged me up to Jake like that."

"Kerry, I…"

"I was so… I felt really stupid. I mean, it must've looked really stupid. You could've gone and asked him without taking me with you…"

"But that was the whole point," Corinne said. "I just thought, you know, that you wouldn't do it yourself, I just wanted to help, that was all. I mean, it was nothing. He plays the guitar, so I asked him to come and play at the party. It's no big deal. Heck, I thought I was giving him an opportunity, an audience, you know."

"Corinne," Kerry sighed, as she turned round. "Zoey says he plays at college. He was probably insulted, being asked to play at a crummy party with a load of kids."

Corinne frowned again. "I don't think so. We're not kids. I just asked and he said 'no'. I was only trying to help."

"I wish you hadn't."

"Why not?"

"Because, if I *was* going to do something like that, I'd like to have done it my way. That's all."

"But you wouldn't..."

"I might've," Kerry said. "But I don't have the chance now. Do I?"

Corinne stood up and faced her. "Kerry, I'm really sorry. It wasn't a big thing. He's not going to dislike you just because you were with me when I asked him to play at Nick's party. I doubt it'll make a difference at all. I mean, face it, if he'd agreed to come, you'd be in heaven now. Wouldn't you?"

"I've never felt so far away from heaven in my life," Kerry snapped.

"Don't let him do that to you," Corinne said, "he's not worth it."

Kerry just shook her head; she thought that he

was. She ran her hands through her long, dark hair. "That's a cliché," she said.

"OK, so it's a cliché. It's also true. I'm sorry, I should've thought first. It was just an impulse. All I was trying to do was to help."

Corinne looked wistful, as if she really was sorry. Kerry gazed at her for a minute, then Corinne smiled, and she smiled back at her. Kerry thought that maybe it was wrong to blame her, it wasn't Corinne's fault that Jake didn't like her.

"Come on," Corinne said, "let's go to Nick's. If you're going to mope, you may as well mope in company."

Kerry tried, but she just couldn't get into the party. The music was good and there were a lot of people there, but the music was too loud to talk and there wasn't anyone she wanted to dance with.

She stood in the hall for a while, and then escaped into the throng in the kitchen when a boy came up to her with a determined look upon his face. Just when she thought she'd got away from him, she turned and found herself face-to-face with him.

He asked her to dance, and he was really mean when she said she didn't want to. That made her feel even worse. Julie and Zoey were there with their boyfriends; she looked at them and wondered if she'd ever have a boyfriend, or if she'd be alone for the rest of her life.

She glanced at her watch, then she grabbed Corinne in between dances.

"I'm going to leave," she said.

"But you can't. It's only just started."

"I'm not in the mood."

Corinne seemed as if she was about to argue, then she changed her mind. "D'you want me to come with you?" she asked.

Kerry shook her head.

It was a relief to be out in the fresh air, away from the crush. The party wasn't bad, it was just a lot of boys looking for girls and vice versa, and, since she'd first seen Jake, Kerry was no longer interested in parties like that.

The evening was warm, still light. Instead of going home, Kerry wandered along the High Street, telling herself that she would get over Jake sometime, she'd meet someone else. The problem was, she didn't know what to do until she got over him, how to get rid of the empty feeling she had inside.

She told herself to stop thinking about him, but it was very hard to do that, he'd been at the centre of her thoughts for a very long time.

"He's just a boy," she told herself, "maybe he's not as nice as he looks…"

"Hello, Kerry," Jake said.

She stopped dead and blinked; it really was him, he was standing just a couple of metres away from her. Kerry was so surprised that she let out a little cry.

"I'm sorry," he said.

Kerry blinked again, and then she told herself to slow down, to talk back to him sensibly.

"It's OK. I was … I was just very deep in thought, that's all."

He grinned, she watched the way his eyes sparkled. "You looked pretty glum."

She blushed, not knowing what to say next.

"You didn't go to the party," he said.

"I did, but it wasn't very good. I left. I thought ... didn't you say you were doing something tonight?"

Kerry blushed then, because she didn't want to sound nosy, but he didn't seem to be upset.

"I am. I wash dishes at the *trattoria* just down the road. Summer job, you know? I'm saving for a new guitar, so I work all the time, just about. I'm really sorry about the party..."

"Oh, no," Kerry said, quickly, "Corinne shouldn't have asked, I mean, you're a professional, you're far too good..."

Jake laughed. "Busking at the mall's about all I do, and the odd gig. I'm not good yet, but I'm trying to get there."

"You will," Kerry blundered. "I really enjoy listening to you."

He winced, and she wondered if she'd said something wrong, but he shook his head.

"It's just that I sent a tape off to a record company," he said, "a demo, you know?"

Kerry didn't, but she nodded anyway.

"The chances are they'll send it straight back again, but I keep on hoping they'll ring up and say they like it. Thing is, it's a one-in-a-million chance, just about. There're thousands of guys out there like me, sending tapes off. I've a better chance of landing on Mars."

She laughed. "I'll keep hoping," she said.

He glanced at his watch, then he frowned. "I have to go," he said.

She hoped the disappointment didn't show on her face.

"It's been nice talking," he said. "I'll see you around."

"Yes," she said. "See you."

Kerry walked home as if she was floating on air. It wasn't until later that she wondered how he'd known her name.

2

Kerry's time at the paper passed in a blur of phone messages and errands; in one hour alone she made six cups of tea and eight mugs of coffee. She was a little surprised when the editor came out of his office and headed for her desk; he usually ignored her, except for a hurried "morning" or a "thank you" when she brought him a pot of tea.

"You want to be a reporter, don't you, Kerry?"

She nodded; she'd told him that when he interviewed her.

"I was just thinking," he said, "things are pretty slow over the summer, so if you've any ideas, write them down and I'll have a look at them."

"What sort of thing d'you want?" she asked, staggered.

He put his hands in his pockets. "Fillers for the feature page, that sort of thing. What young people are doing, anything unusual or interesting. That piece you did about the boy with cerebral palsy becoming a sculptor, the one that won the competition, that was just great."

Without thinking, Kerry told him about Jake playing in the mall, trying to get a recording contract.

"I don't know," he said, "that's what they all do, isn't it? I mean, every kid that can play two chords together thinks he's the next John Lennon."

"I don't know about John Lennon," Kerry said, "but Jake's really good."

"Do it," the editor said. "About 300 words, but put an interesting spin on it. Not 'local-boy-headed-for-stardom', try to make it snappy and witty."

"OK," Kerry said.

After the editor left, she realized that Jake might not want her to write about him, but if she didn't do the piece, the editor would be upset.

Kerry sighed, and went off to fill the tea urn.

"Umm," Zoey said, after Kerry had told her all about it when they met for a coffee after work. "All you can do is ask Jake, I suppose."

"But what if he says no?" Kerry moaned.

"If he's got any sense, he won't."

Corinne flopped down, and asked them what they were talking about. Kerry told her.

"So I did help, after all," she said.

Kerry nodded. "Maybe," she said.

She spent the next two days working out how exactly to ask Jake when she saw him again on Wednesday, but when the time came, she still wasn't ready.

She waited nervously outside the mall, praying that he'd arrive with time to talk to her, checking her watch every few minutes. At last, she saw him walking along, just five minutes before he had to begin his spot.

"Hi," she said.

"Hello," he smiled.

"I was wondering," she began, "I'm working on the *Gazette* during the summer, and the editor said, I mean, I was thinking, it'd be nice if I could write a story about you. It might not help, but they say that all publicity's good publicity…" Her voice tailed off as she realized that she was talking far too fast, but his smile had broadened into a grin.

"That'd be great," he said.

"It might not make the paper, it probably won't, but they want to run some stories about young people over the summer, and I thought it would be nice to talk to you first."

"OK…"

"So if we could have a chat some time, just so that I can get some background, I mean, how you got into music, how you made the demo tape and so on."

He brushed his hair back. "How about after I finish? I start at the *trattoria* at eight, but I'm free until then."

"Fine," Kerry said, wondering if she could bear to wait until then.

At last, Jake finished singing. The others had left, leaving Kerry alone with him.

He sat down, wiping the sheen from his forehead. He looked so gorgeous that Kerry's heart fluttered.

"Let me get you something to drink," she said nervously, unsure how to begin.

"No. I'll get you something."

"I'm interviewing you."

"Yes, but I need to impress you, don't I?"

She laughed, and asked for a mineral water. The coffee bar at the mall was expensive and she didn't want to waste his money.

"So, what d'you want to know?" he asked, once he'd got the drinks.

Kerry took out the little tape recorder she'd bought and switched it on.

"Let's start with how you got started, why music means so much to you."

He nodded. "How I got started? Well, according to my mother, when I was a baby, I used to shake my rattle in time with the radio."

"Really?"

"She says so. Apparently, there was some music I liked, and some I didn't."

"What do you like?"

"Almost everything, but I don't like what I think of as commercial pop. You know, these groups that are put together by managers, they all sound alike. It sounds too much like music made to make money, it hasn't got soul, not the way that music made for music's sake has. Does that make any sense?"

"I s'pose," Kerry said.

Jake rubbed his forehead. "You'd better not say

that, because it'll upset the record companies. They all do it, packaged commercial pop. If they read me saying something like that, they'll say, who is this guy? I'll have less of a chance than I have now."

Kerry laughed. "What do I say then?"

He thought for a moment. "I don't really know. Maybe something about music being a great way to communicate. But that sounds cruddy, doesn't it? I don't know, say what you want to say. I grew up with music. Other people, when they think back, they might remember a game or a toy. I remember pop songs, the good ones, that is."

"The non-commercial, non-packaged ones?"

"I guess so. The thing is, at the moment, the record companies spend a lot of time trying to copy sounds that have been successful, and not enough time on the kind of new stuff that's exciting and different. Say Band A has a hit single, another record company will get Band B to do the same thing, and so on and so on. So what you have is a lot of people copying each other, so instead of developing it's going around in circles."

Kerry chewed her pencil. "They'd be really fed up if you say that."

He shrugged. "It's true."

"So, what do you want to do with music?"

He thought for a moment, rubbed his neck. "That's tough. It's something I don't really talk about. I love playing music, my own music, I mean, but I don't know if I'll make it. Right now, I'm trying to get the money for a new guitar, at least, a good second-hand one. So I'm working pretty much all of the time."

"What about the tape you sent off?"

He winced. "What about it? It's a couple of songs I recorded at college that I decided to send off. Chances are, it'll come back like a boomerang. But I decided to try."

"Who did you send it to?"

"An independent label – that's a record company – in London," he said. "It's called Reflex. I read in a music paper that they listen to every tape that comes in, so I sent it. Y'see, most labels, they only listen to the first few bars, but Reflex say they listen to the whole track..." He brushed his hair back, and began to talk about the music business, the way it was dominated by Sony and Warner, the way all the money went into the big bands and acts, with only a little left for all the others. He said music was becoming more and more like any other business, as if the music itself was just a sideline, a product, a way to make money like selling cans of baked beans.

Kerry was fascinated, because he really knew what he was talking about, and he passionately believed in making music for music's sake. She realized then that it didn't matter to him if he wound up as a busker, like Corinne had said; all that mattered was that he was able to make the music he wanted to make.

She listened intently to every single word, nodding as she agreed with it, not wanting to say anything because she didn't want him to stop. Her tape ran out with a little click, but she ignored it, because she couldn't bear to interrupt the flow.

After a long time he sat back and stretched. "I'm

boring you," he said, with a sad little smile.

"Not at all," she said. All she wanted him to do then was to go on talking for ever and ever.

He brushed his hair back again, and she found herself wanting to brush it back for him.

Oops, she thought, I'm falling in love.

Correction: I *have fallen* in love.

He looked at his watch and frowned. "It's nearly eight. I'm late for the *trattoria*."

She hadn't even noticed people leaving: the coffee bar was on the point of closing down.

They got up and walked out into the soft summer evening. She'd missed dinner, would have to find an explanation, but she wasn't even thinking about that.

"Well, it's been nice talking," he said.

"I'll write it up and let the editor see it," she said. "I hope he puts it in the paper, but he might not."

Jake shrugged. "Thanks for listening anyway," he said. "So long."

"Yes," she said. "So long."

Kerry struggled late into the night to turn Jake's words into a story that made sense. In despair, she gave up just before midnight, setting her alarm for six so she could try again early the next day.

An idea came to her in her sleep; in the morning, she wrote a brief story which she called *Music for Music's Sake* all about the various jobs that Jake was doing so that he could buy a new guitar. She didn't mention his comments about the music business, she only said in passing that he'd sent a demo tape to one of the London record companies.

At work, she printed the story neatly and put it on the editor's desk, then she waited nervously. Nothing happened for days; at first she put it down to the looming deadline, then she supposed the editor wasn't interested. She was so embarrassed that she didn't go to the mall on Wednesday.

Since she'd spoken to Jake a few days ago, her life had turned into a roller-coaster of thrills followed by troughs of deep despair.

On Friday, she was about to leave the office, when a photographer strolled up to her desk. "Where's this guy Jake Michaels?" he asked, yawning. "I need a colour pic for the Midweek Diary."

Kerry's stomach lurched. "He plays in the mall at five," she said.

"Right, I'll get him there."

"I'll come with you."

"You don't need to, darling. I'm a big boy, I can manage on my own."

Kerry flushed crimson.

The story ran in the paper's midweek edition. Kerry's headline had been changed to: *A Star in the Making?*

Oh, no, she thought, sure that she had upset Jake deeply.

At the mall that afternoon, Kerry was silent.

"What's up?" Zoey asked her.

"It's the story I wrote about Jake," she said, "the headline was such a cliché. I don't think he'll like it."

"You don't know that," Zoey said.

"Yes, but I'm worried about it. You know?"

"I know."

Zoey smiled; Kerry smiled back at her. She felt bad about the story, so bad that she left the mall just after Jake began his spot, sure that he was annoyed with her.

Jake read the story, then he read it again, smiling to himself. He wasn't too happy about the headline, but she'd been really careful not to mention anything that would upset the record companies, and at the same time she'd said that he believed in music for music's sake.

He felt such a fool, because he'd had the perfect chance to ask her out, but he'd muffed it.

The thing was, he had so little time, and even less money; it seemed pretty lame to just ask her to come for a walk along the river, or maybe a coffee on the odd night that he got off from the *trattoria*, because he couldn't afford anything more.

He wasn't sure that she liked him, and he didn't want to risk being turned down. Like his last girl-friend had said, he wasn't exactly the catch of the century. He didn't have any money, and he spent most of his time working on songs.

That remark had hurt Jake, although he knew the girl wasn't right for him. She had ambitions and drive that he didn't share, although he had ambitions of his own; when they split up she'd starting going out with a boy with a lot of money and a car of his own.

But Kerry was different, he sensed that. Although she hadn't been in the mall one day and had then left before he finished his spot the next, there was something between them, he was pretty sure of it.

She stayed on his mind all the time, as he washed dishes at the *trattoria,* and then in the mornings when he sorted the mail. As he played music, he was thinking of her eyes, her smile, the way her head turned slightly to one side as she listened to him.

The tune came to him out of nowhere. He strummed a few chords and then a few more, then he had the song; all he needed was the words.

The girl with the smile in her eyes, he thought, then he sang it, just like that, and it worked.

He worked on the song for a while, humming the tune as he washed dishes, putting the words together in his head as he sorted mail and then delivered leaflets in the afternoon for a few extra pounds.

When he put it all together, he taped it; when he played it back he realized that it was the best thing he'd ever written.

He wanted so much to play it to her, for her to like it as much as he did, but he wasn't sure, was afraid of taking the risk.

Besides, although he knew her full name now, Kerry Smith, there were at least a thousand of them in the phone book, and he didn't know which one was her.

Jake went to the mall on Wednesday afternoon early; Kerry's friends weren't there yet, only the blonde one he didn't particularly like. He waited hesitantly at the entrance on the High Street, thinking she was sure to come that way because the newspaper's office was just along the road.

Sure enough, she appeared, walking briskly with her head down, so that she didn't notice him.

She jumped when he stood in front of her and said, "Hello."

"Jake," she said, in a voice that was flat and dull.

"I ... I just wanted to thank you for the story," he said. "It was really terrific."

"I didn't write the headline," she said quickly. "That was the editor, not me."

He shook his head. "It was really good, the way you said what I thought about music, without saying anything rude."

She looked flustered. "I just said what you said, that's all."

"I've got to do my spot now—"

"Yes," she said, quickly. "See you."

Then she turned and walked away.

3

Jake swallowed the hurt that he felt, then he began to play. He'd been about to say that, if she had time, they could have a coffee later, when he finished his spot, but she'd gone before he had a chance.

There was something brittle about her, as if he'd done something to upset her, but he wasn't sure what. He hadn't had a chance to do much with her; maybe he'd bored her rotten by going on about music like that.

His last girlfriend had accused him of being more interested in the music business than he was in her; he'd started to argue, then stopped when he realized that she was right. When she'd seen the look on his face, she'd said some pretty nasty things that had hurt him a lot; in revenge, he supposed, because he didn't like her that much.

But Kerry wasn't like that; he was as interested in her as he was in his music. For Jake, that was really something. He wondered what to do about it, whether he could do anything because he'd so little time and money and hardly anything at all to offer a girl like her. She was good-looking and kind and witty, her long brown hair shone like polished mahogany, and her eyes were deep amber pools that he longed to dive into.

He finished the song he was playing, was about to begin another when he noticed Mrs Brown waving at him. She always put money in the box, and she liked Simon and Garfunkel, so he waved back and then began *Bridge Over Troubled Water*. As he played, he wondered if she knew how hard it was to adapt a song written for piano to the guitar, how long he had practised to get it right. The way she smiled at him when he finished, though, told him that she appreciated it.

He glanced at Kerry, saw her deep in conversation with her friends. Fleetingly, he wondered if she was still aware of him. Automatically, his fingers began to play the chords of the song he had written about her. The lyrics weren't right yet, only the chorus, he would have to play it mostly instrumentally, singing just a line or two.

He cleared his throat. He had to play it now he had started, if he stopped the audience would notice that something was wrong.

"This is a song I wrote for somebody I met recently," he said, humming the tune until he came to the chorus.

"The girl with the smile in her eyes."

As Jake began to sing, Kerry's stomach turned

over. For an instant, she thought the song might be about her, then she told herself to stop dreaming. He hardly even knew her; he was just being nice when he thanked her for the story.

He'd had a chance to ask her out, and he hadn't bothered, so he wasn't interested.

Face facts, she told herself.

Apart from anything else, that time they'd talked in the mall, he told her that he wrote songs about anything, people he saw in the street, even strangers. *The girl with the smile in her eyes* was a girl he'd seen and liked from a distance, without knowing anything about her.

Kerry felt a rush of jealousy for this unknown muse; she wondered who she was, if she'd any idea of how much pain she caused, was causing right now.

Corinne finished telling a story, and Zoey and Julie laughed.

Corinne laughed too, and tossed her blonde hair back. She had beautiful blue eyes, the colour of a summer sky.

It's her, Kerry thought, as her stomach dropped ten thousand feet. Corinne's the girl with the smile in her eyes. All the boys she knew were mad about Corinne. It stood to reason that Jake was as well.

Zoey looked at her. "Why so glum?"

"I shouldn't've written that story about Jake. I'm really embarrassed about it."

Zoey nodded as if she understood.

Corinne stood up to go. "Have to rush," she said. "Hot date tonight."

Kerry walked home slowly with Zoey.

"You've gone all quiet," Zoey said, after a while.

Kerry sighed. "I think Jake's fallen for Corinne."

Zoey stopped walking and turned to look at her. "Why?"

"Well, that song. *The Girl With The Smile In Her Eyes*. It's about Corinne. It has to be. She's got gorgeous eyes."

Zoey gazed at her. "You've got nice eyes too, Kerry."

"I don't. They're brown and boring."

"No, they aren't. They're deep and soulful. And they light up when you smile. It could just as easily be about you. In fact, I think it *is* about you."

"Why?"

"A couple of times, I saw Jake looking at you. He kept on looking at you."

"He could have been looking at Corinne. She was right beside me."

Zoey winced, exasperated. "Kerry, get into the real world. You're just as pretty as Corinne. You're different, that's all. And looks aren't everything. You're a really nice person. That counts for an awful lot."

Kerry shrugged. She wished that she could believe what Zoey said. "Jake's probably got a girlfriend, anyway. I mean, he had a chance to ask me out. When I interviewed him for the story, we talked for ages, then he just said, 'See you'."

Zoey frowned. "He's never with anyone at the mall. I could ask Chris if he's seeing someone."

"Oh, could you?"

"Sure," Zoey said.

When Kerry got home, she looked at herself in the mirror. She studied her reflection every which way, smiling, frowning, straight-faced. She brushed her hair back, forward, shook her head so that it hung naturally.

Zoey's right, she decided, after an age. I might not be drop-dead gorgeous, but I'm not that bad.

Zoey came round on Saturday afternoon. "Jake had a girlfriend but they split up a while ago," she said.

"D'you know who she was?" Kerry asked her. She'd put a wax treatment on her hair to make it shine, and she had to keep her hair wrapped in a towel for an hour.

Zoey shook her head. "Chris doesn't know him that well. They're doing different courses."

Kerry sighed deeply.

"What's the matter?"

"I just don't know enough about him, Zoey. I mean, when I talk to him, we seem to get on well, but all he ever says is, 'See you'. He never says when. I just don't know if he likes me or not."

"I think he likes you," Zoey said. "If he didn't like you, he wouldn't've bothered to talk to you in the first place. It sounds like he's got a lot to do with his time. He's not going to waste time on somebody he's not interested in, is he?"

"Oh, Zoey, I don't know. I don't know what he thinks, that's the whole trouble."

"Apart from anything else," Zoey said, "I don't suppose it's dawned on you that he might be shy."

"Shy?"

"Shy, Kerry. S.H.Y. Lots of boys are shy. Chris's shy. Simon's so shy that it took him two months to work up the courage to ask me out."

"Two months? I'll go mad if I have to wait that long."

Zoey laughed. "Come on, you've only known him for a few days."

"Yes, but I've been crazy about him for ages."

"Give him a little more time," Zoey said. "Just be yourself."

Kerry went to rinse the wax out of her hair and make some coffee. She had been thinking, vaguely, of asking Jake for a coffee, but when she'd seen him at the mall, she'd been so embarrassed about the story she hadn't dared; she'd just gone away as quickly as she could.

When she got back, Zoey had a wistful expression on her face.

"You know," she said, "I envy you, in a way."

"Why?"

"It's so exciting, just when you're starting to get to know somebody. Just think of the thrill when you do go out with him. Just think of the first kiss."

Kerry felt dizzy at the idea of it. She had to tell herself that it might never happen. "But you're happy with Simon, aren't you, Zoey?"

"Yes and no. It's nice to have a boyfriend, in a way, but sometimes... I mean, we're not Romeo and Juliet." She didn't say any more and Kerry realized that she did not want to talk about it.

Corinne came round later. Her hot date had gone icy cold. He'd been wearing a brand of cologne that she hated, and he'd clamped his hand on her knee as soon as the film started. "I mean, *yuck!*" she said. "We didn't even hold hands or anything first. And he had a spot on his chin."

They spent the evening watching videos, with Corinne freeze-framing on the close-ups of the actors she fancied.

Despite Zoey's reassurances, Kerry couldn't help thinking that maybe Corinne was the one that Jake liked, after all.

"Corinne," she said, slowly, "do you like Jake at all? Even a little bit?"

Corinne was deeply involved in a study of a pair of eyes that she swore were the greenest she had ever seen. "Told you," she said, "he's not my type."

On Monday, at work, two of the reporters had gone down with summer flu, so Kerry spent the entire day glued to the phone, taking messages, while the news editor tried to write all the stories himself.

"You did really well," he said, at the end of the day, when the phones were silent at last. It was after six, Kerry'd had to stay late, so she hadn't met up with the others in the mall. "Can you come in early tomorrow morning and stay on again? You'll get paid for it, of course."

"Sure," Kerry said. She could use the extra money.

The next day, the phone rang when she was having a late lunch. She picked it up tiredly – it had been going constantly all morning and she had been trying to eat a cheese sandwich.

"Hello?" she said.

"Can I speak to Kerry Smith, please?" a male voice said.

Her heart skipped a beat. It was Jake.

"Yes. I mean, it's me."

"Hi, Kerry. The reason I'm ringing is that I've just had a call from Reflex Records."

Kerry had to think for a moment before she realized that he was talking about the record company that he'd sent his tape too. "Yes?" she said, nervously; she wanted so much for things to go well for him.

"They're not offering me a contract yet, but they want me to go into the studio and make a proper demo, with session guys doing the backing."

"Is that good?"

"It's great. The tape I sent in, the mixing isn't so good. The guy who rang, he said he wants a really good demo to play to this meeting they're having. Y'see, it's not just him who makes the decision, it's his boss as well. But he sounded really positive about it, he said he hopes they're going to be able to offer me something. At the very least, I'll have a really good demo tape."

"I see," she said, slowly. She didn't really.

Jake cleared his throat. "The reason I rang is," he said, "that I was thinking, maybe you'd like to come with me..."

Kerry blinked and gripped the receiver tightly. He'd asked her out, he had actually asked her out. She was so happy that she had to suppress the urge to jump up and shout.

"...I thought," he went on, "that it would be a really good story for you to do for the *Gazette*, you know, going into a proper recording studio and watching how a record's made."

She was a little disappointed that he'd mentioned the paper. "I don't know," she said, "I mean, I don't know if the editor would be interested. I'd have to ask him. But I'd really like to come."

"Well, it's this Thursday," he said. "We'll get the eight a.m. train to London. I'm taking the day off work."

Kerry frowned. Thursday was the busiest day at the paper, this week would be absolutely frantic because so many people were off sick. "I'm … I'm not sure if I can get the time off, Jake. It's press day, you see. I'll ask, and I'll ring you back, OK?"

"OK," Jake said. "I'm just on my way out to do some leafleting. I'll be in between half-seven and eight."

"I'll ring you then," Kerry said.

The afternoon passed in a flash. Kerry did not get a chance to talk to the editor until after the office closed at six o'clock. He listened to her request in silence, then slowly shook his head.

"I'm sorry, Kerry," he said. "If it was a normal week, I'd said, yes, no problem, but you know how it's been. There're big stories breaking and half the staff are off with flu. In any case, it's not as if he's actually got a recording contract."

"Yes, but", she said, "it would be interesting to watch a demo being made."

"Not interesting enough," he said, firmly, before his face relaxed into a smile and he told her how well she was coping with the extra work, that he didn't know what he would do without her. She said that she didn't do much, she just answered the phones and took messages; he said that if she wasn't around to do that, the constantly ringing phones would drive him mad.

Kerry walked home slowly, thinking all the way. It's only a job, she told herself, I could always just quit. There were other jobs; she might manage to get one at the supermarket, but it wouldn't be nearly as much fun. It was strange, really, how much the job on the paper had meant to her when she first got it, how little it meant now that it kept her away from seeing Jake.

Then again, she thought, it wasn't as if he had actually asked her for a date. It wasn't as if he'd said, "I'd like you to come with me." The way he put it was more tentative than that. Yet Zoey had said that he might be shy, maybe he needed an excuse to ask her out. Whatever she did, she didn't want him to get the idea that she didn't like him. But she didn't want to give up her job on the paper to spend the rest of the summer stacking shelves, or, worse, doing nothing at all and trying to survive on the little she'd saved.

The dilemma whirled around in her mind for ages. Seven-thirty came, and she still hadn't come to a decision.

In torment, she tried to ring Zoey, but she was out with Simon. Corinne answered on the first ring. "Don't be crazy," she said. "You'll get another chance of a job. You might not get another chance of Jake."

That was it, Corinne had put it succinctly.

Kerry picked up the phone and punched out Jake's number.

"Kerry," he said, "I was just on my way out to work. Can you come?"

She opened her mouth to say yes, then remembered what the editor had said that afternoon, about how they couldn't manage without her, now that everybody was off with flu. Like all the other staff, he'd been kind to her, patiently explaining how things worked. It just wouldn't be right to leave him in the lurch, not after he had given her the job which so many others had wanted.

"I wish I could, Jake, but most of the staff are off ill with flu. I can't get the time off."

"I see," he said.

"I'd feel awful about it if I just came anyway, without permission. They've all been so nice to me and it would be like I was betraying their trust."

"I understand," he said.

"If it was any other time," she said, lamely. "If you *do* get the contract, he'll want me to do a story about it."

"Kerry, I understand. Really, I do. I have to work pretty hard myself. I know what it's like."

"I'm dying to know how you get on. Will you tell me?"

"Sure. I'll see you in the mall, won't I?"

"Yes. Of course."

"Well, thanks for ringing. I have to go now, or I'll be late for work."

Kerry put the phone down, feeling rotten but knowing that she would've felt worse if she had left her job and gone anyway.

She'd hoped so much that he would make a definite arrangement to meet her. He'd sounded so vague about seeing her in the mall.

4

Jake put the clean dish on the rack to dry, then picked up the new pile of dirty ones and dropped them into the soapy water. He kept on telling himself that this was the late 20th century, it was a waste of human resources to wash dishes manually, but Mario, the owner of the Italian *trattoria* where he worked, didn't think so.

Mario thought that he was doing Jake a great favour by employing him; Jake grinned as he realized that his boss really *was* doing him a favour, because without the dishwashing job, he wouldn't be able to afford the second-hand Stratocaster that he'd seen in the music shop. He'd put a deposit on it the other day, as soon as he had seen it. In another few weeks, it would be his.

Jake tried to think of the guitar to keep his mind off Kerry. Although she sounded sincere, and he understood she had to work, because he had to work himself, he was disappointed that she couldn't come with him. Because she'd turned him down, it made it a bit more difficult to ask her out. The way he'd planned it, they'd spend the day at the studio in London and then, on the train home, he'd explain it all to her; that he had only a little free time and even less money, but he'd like to spend the time he had with her.

Thinking about it, everything sounded so lame, as if he was the jerk of the week. He liked Kerry, he wanted to ask her out, but he couldn't. OK, so there were *real* problems such as his lack of time and money, but he could think of a dozen ways around them like he could borrow his brother's inflatable and take her for a row along the river, or he could barbecue some burgers in the back garden that was never used now that his brothers and sisters had grown up. Although he didn't like to admit it to himself, the truth was that Jake was afraid that Kerry would reject him. In a way, it was maybe better for his music to keep at a distance, so that in his yearning for her he could write more really good songs.

When he went to do the demo, he planned to play *Kerry's Song*, the tune he'd written for her the day after he'd spoken to her. As he finished the pile of dishes, he began to hum it as he put them on the rack to dry and then started on some freshly dirty ones.

"Ees nice tune," Mario said, as he came into the kitchen with some dirty pots. The *trattoria* was a family business; Mario and his wife cooked, his brother managed the restaurant, and several of his nephews and nieces waited on the tables.

"I wrote it myself," Jake said, shyly.

"Molto bene," Mario said. Although he'd lived in England for twenty-five years, he'd never become used to the language. "Ees love song, yes?"

Jake flushed.

"Eyah," said Mario, happily. "You look like you're een love."

Jake said nothing, wiping his brow with his forearm to try to make out that it was the heat that made him so red.

"You bring 'er for meal," Mario said. "I geeve you special price, deescount."

"I haven't time," Jake said tersely. "I work every night you're open."

"Always time for love," Mario said. "Always make time for love. Deeshes can wait. Love cannot."

Furiously, Jake picked up a cloth and began to wipe the dishes waiting in the drying rack.

Kerry spent all day Thursday on tenterhooks. All she could think of was Jake, that he was making his demo now. It was make-or-break for him; she knew that. He'd been on her mind all the time since she'd rung on Tuesday. She couldn't help thinking that she should have gone with him, despite the problems at the paper, that, maybe, she'd blown the only chance that she'd get.

Once all the films and the disks had gone to the printer's, the editor congratulated her; three stories that she had written were in the paper, one was actually on the front page. A week ago, Kerry would have been delighted. Today, she hardly cared.

In the mall with Zoey and Corinne, she sat

listening as they talked about Julie and Mike. They'd been going out for three years now, they wanted to go on holiday together and Julie's parents had decided to let her.

"I mean," Zoey said, "it's really serious. It's not as if they'd just met. I think they'll get engaged soon. Julie said they've talked about it, but Mike wants to wait until he's finished college."

Corinne shrugged.

"Aren't you excited?" Zoey asked her.

"You date one boy for ages and then you marry him. That's exciting?"

Zoey laughed. "It's exciting to be thinking of getting married."

"Yeah?" Corinne stretched in her seat. "I want to have some fun first. And when I do marry, it won't be someone boring like Mike."

"Who will it be?" Zoey asked her.

"Oh, I don't know. A rock star, a Hollywood actor..."

"They're mostly married already, or in a committed relationship, as they say."

"So what's a little competition? Each girl for herself, I say."

Zoey laughed again. "What about you, Kerry?"

Kerry started at the mention of her name. She'd been miles away.

"Who'd you like to marry?"

Kerry blushed furiously. The first thought that came into her mind was that she would like to marry Jake, but she couldn't say that. Zoey caught her discomfort and quickly changed the subject to the bus that was running from Alton directly to the Music Channel Summer Party at the Wembley Stadium. The biggest stars in rock and pop were going to be there. As a reward for all her hard work, the editor had given Kerry a pair of tickets that the promoters had sent to the paper, but she didn't really want them. She'd wanted to go to the party only if Jake would go with her.

For a moment, she thought of asking him, then she remembered that he worked in the *trattoria*, and she was afraid that he'd turn her down.

Corinne sighed deeply. "It's booked up already. I went to get tickets and they were sold out. Dad tried to get some in London, but they were sold out there too."

"I'd rather go to a movie," Zoey said.

"Zoey, how can you?" Corinne wailed. "At a concert, they're all there, in the flesh. You can just about reach out and touch the boy of your dreams. He might notice you and fall madly in love."

They all laughed.

"I've got tickets," Kerry said. "You can have them if you like."

"Ohh, can I?" Corinne said. "I'll pay for them."

Kerry shook her head. "I got them for free." She took the tickets out of her bag and handed them to Corinne, who kissed them and then sighed deeply. "Maybe this is the beginning of my first love affair," she said.

On the way home, Zoey asked Kerry what the matter was. "You hardly said anything in the mall," she said, "and you've been really quiet all week."

Kerry thought for a moment. "Would you like to come back to my place for a pizza?" she asked Zoey. "My parents are out till late, and my mother always leaves one in the fridge for me."

"Sure," Zoey said.

Over a pepperoni with extra cheese, Kerry told her all about how Jake had asked her to go to the demo with her, and how she felt she had to refuse because of her obligation to the paper.

"Jeez," Zoey said, once she'd finished, "I see what you mean."

"What would you have done?" Kerry asked her.

"I don't know. I think I'd do what you did. It's not like you had much choice."

"But there're other jobs," Kerry said, echoing Corinne. "I might not get another chance with Jake."

"I don't think it's like that," Zoey said. "It's not as if you're dating already. From what you've told me, I think Jake's the kind of guy who'd understand about the paper. I think he'd respect you for that."

"But you said you thought he was shy."

"I do. That just means he's more sensitive, more likely to understand. As long as you didn't make it sound like a put-down."

Kerry thought again, for the millionth time, over what she'd said.

"I don't think so," she said, slowly. "He *said* he understood."

"Well then," Zoey said brightly.

"I don't suppose you could ask your brother about his old girlfriend? I mean, if he was really cut up about her, or if he didn't care that much."

Zoey shook her head. "Like I said, Chris doesn't

know him that well. I asked all I could, and he starting asking me, why did I want to know?"

"I see."

"You'll just have to find out for yourself."

Kerry moaned. "I know. I keep on thinking, maybe I should ring him and ask how he got on, but I don't want to, I don't want to..."

"You don't want to what?"

"Well, when Corinne meets a new boy, she's all over him, and I think sometimes she smothers them."

"Yeah," Zoey said. "I know. That's why her boy-friends never last very long."

"The thing is," Kerry said, "whatever I do, I don't want to do that."

When Zoey left, Kerry's hand hovered over the phone, as if attracted by magnetism. She dialled Jake's number several times, then put the receiver down quickly after the last digit.

"This is stupid," she said, to herself. She had a perfect reason to ring him, she could even pretend that she was interested on the paper's behalf.

Kerry picked up the phone again, dialled the number and then waited as it rang.

"Hello?" a voice said, that of an older woman.

It must be Jake's mother, she thought.

"Can I speak to Jake?" she said.

"Jake's at the *trattoria*, but I'll give him a message, if you like."

"No," said Kerry quickly, cursing herself for forgetting that Jake left for work before eight o'clock. "No message."

I'll see him at the mall tomorrow, she thought.

On Friday, Kerry waited outside the coffee bar; she didn't want to sit at a table yet, she wanted to make sure that she had a moment or two with Jake first. Although Zoey would understand, Corinne might not and she did not want to take the chance that she would butt in.

It was ten to five before Jake came through the automatic doors with his guitar case in one hand and a music bag in the other.

Kerry's heart jumped when she saw him, as it always did, but as he walked towards her, she saw that he was frowning, his brow furrowed in deep lines.

"Hi," she said, suppressing the urge to ask him how it had gone. If the demo had gone well, he'd tell her himself, and if it hadn't, she didn't want to embarrass him.

"Hi, Kerry," he said, smiling.

She looked at him and he looked at her; for a moment, neither of them spoke.

"I don't know yet," he said, "about the demo, I mean."

She nodded.

"It went, well, it felt as if it went well, but I did a new song, and I'm not sure if it was ready yet, the arrangement, I mean."

"What was the studio like?"

He grinned broadly. "It was amazing. Nothing like the one at college. There was an engineer on the mixing deck and another one who actually cut the master tape. And the backing guys, they were tremendous. I just gave them the score and they played it as if they'd been practising for ages. One of them was really nice. Over lunch, he told me all about the business. He really liked my songs, said they were original, not the sort of copied stuff that makes the charts."

Kerry smiled. "So it's looking good?"

Jake winced. "It's looking so-so. The guy at Reflex, he phoned this afternoon. He says the demo's good. He wants to offer me a contract for a single, but he has to get it passed at this meeting they're having next week…"

"When next week?"

"I don't know. I was so amazed he liked it that I didn't ask. But he said he'll let me know for sure next week. Until then, well…" He smiled nervously. "I guess it's sweating blood time."

Kerry didn't know what to say. It was nearly five o'clock, the folk singers had finished their spot and it was time for him to go on.

"I'll let you know," he said, as he began to walk towards the stand.

Kerry called him back. "Jake?"

"Yes?"

"I'll keep my fingers crossed," she said.

5

Kerry stared glumly into her cappuccino. It was Monday afternoon; she'd spent the weekend watching videos and thinking about Jake, because Corinne had a new boyfriend who she'd met at the country club who she said was really dreamy. She was away buying a new dress now, for a date tomorrow. She'd seen the dress on the way to the coffee bar and then spent ten minutes wondering whether to buy it or not. Her father had given her a credit card "for emergencies". It didn't take Corinne long to decide that a date with her new boyfriend was an emergency.

"You've gone all quiet again," Zoey said.

Kerry sighed; she felt a little guilty because she knew she was bad company these days.

"It's Jake," she said. "He'll hear about his contract this week, whether he's got it or not. He's really worried about it."

Zoey smiled. "You're worried too."

"He'll be really disappointed if he doesn't get it."

Zoey took a sip of her coffee. "He's still very young, isn't he? I mean, young to get a recording contract? Most of them are, what, in their mid-twenties, and they've only been around for a year or two. So Jake's got plenty of time. And he's got talent. If he doesn't get this one, there'll be other chances."

That makes sense, Kerry thought, but she doubted that Jake would see it like that.

"You're still worried that you won't get another chance with him," Zoey said.

Kerry looked away. "Yes," she said.

"If he's got any sense, you will," Zoey said.

Corinne came back then, plonking the carrier bag with the dress in it down on the spare chair, because Julie was away on holiday with her boyfriend.

"It cost a fortune," she said, laughing, "Dad'll blow a fuse."

Tuesday and Wednesday passed achingly slowly at the paper. The staff who'd been ill had recovered from the flu, and Kerry was relegated to making coffee and taking messages again. Although she still got a thrill from working in a newspaper office, she became bored because she knew she could do so much more than she was doing.

The only good thing was that the editor told her to make sure she applied in the autumn for the trainee's job that would start next year, when she left school.

On Wednesday at three, Kerry rushed home and

washed her hair, then she dressed carefully in a tight white top and her new black Levis, with black leather lace-ups. Shaking her still-damp hair, she studied her reflection in the mirror, thought that she would do. If she had Corinne's money, she'd buy designer clothes from the expensive boutique in the mall; because she didn't, she had to make do with the chain stores and a little imagination. She smiled to herself as she realized that things could be much worse.

Corinne *did* have her good points, she was generous with her castoffs and, if it hadn't been for Corinne, Kerry would probably still be gazing at Jake from a distance.

Kerry picked up her backpack and ran out of the door. It was twenty to five, and she didn't want to be late.

With any luck, she thought, as she walked towards the mall, Jake will know. With any luck, it'll be good news.

She was sure of his talent, sure that, sooner or later, he *would* succeed, but, for his sake, she wanted it to be now.

There was the squeak of brakes being sharply applied. Kerry looked up and saw, straight ahead of her, a Mercedes going slam bang into a Golf that was angling its way out of a parking space.

As soon as the cars had collided, the door of the Mercedes opened and a man got out, shaking his fist at the driver of the Golf. Kerry smiled to herself, it was a typical Alton bump, anywhere else the cars would be mundane and a few years old; in Alton, they were brand-new and expensive.

The driver of the Golf was edging across the passenger seat; she couldn't get out of her own door because the Mercedes had impacted it. She got out and glared angrily at the Mercedes driver.

"You were going too fast," she said.

"The hell I was! You didn't look where you were going!"

"I did! The road was clear! You came out of nowhere!"

Kerry laughed and stopped at the pedestrian lights to cross the street. Suddenly, her arm was grabbed from behind. She turned around and saw the woman who'd been in the passenger seat of the Mercedes.

"You saw what happened," she snapped. "You're a witness."

Kerry sighed and glanced at her watch. It was ten to five; she didn't have the time.

"I'll give you my address," she said.

"No," the woman said. "You'll have to wait. I've called the police on the mobile. They'll be here in a minute."

Kerry jerked her arm free. "I haven't got time," she said.

The woman's face softened. "Please," she said. "You saw what happened. It's Jack's first good car and it's brand-new. It'll only take a minute or two."

"I didn't really see it," Kerry said. "I only saw when they hit each other." She opened her bag and began to write down her name and address.

The police arrived then. The station was only a couple of hundred metres down the road.

"This is a witness," the woman said, triumphantly.

"Right, miss," the policeman said. "Let's have your details."

Jake looked around for a final time, realizing with an ache that was almost physical that Kerry wasn't there. He'd been so keen to see her; she'd been the first person he'd thought of after the phone call from Reflex Records that had told him he was being offered a contract to do a single with an option to do an album if the single went well. The details had blurred; he hadn't listened to the talk of money or clauses, all he'd thought about was the look he'd see on Kerry's face when he told her the good news.

But she wasn't there.

Oh, well, he thought, as he checked the tuning of his guitar, she probably doesn't care. She was probably just being kind. He'd rung her at the paper, but she'd already left, and he *still* didn't have her home phone number.

It was a pity, because he was going to record the single, the song he'd written for her, next week; he'd wanted to ask her to come to the recording with him. She said the editor wanted her to do a story if he got the contract, and when he'd phoned the paper he'd found out that the flu outbreak was over.

When he'd heard about the contract, his father had lent him the rest of the money he needed to pay for the second-hand Stratocaster he'd seen in the Alton music shop. The guitar was the stuff of

Jake's dreams, it played beautifully. When he'd bought it two hours ago he couldn't wait to get to the mall, to play it properly. But Kerry wasn't there, and her absence took the edge off his joy.

She walked in ten minutes later. She looked flustered, out of breath. Jake felt his heart lift when she gave him a tiny wave and smiled that smile of hers. He was too professional to interrupt his spot; he'd have to wait for the end. He felt a thrill when he played the next chord.

Kerry sighed. "You wouldn't believe it," she said, as she began to tell them about the crash and the woman and the police.

Zoey smiled sympathetically. "Jake looks happy," she whispered, after Kerry had finished her story.

Kerry had noticed that, but she didn't dare to hope.

Corinne bought the coffees and then began to tell them about her date. He was a bit older than her, twenty-one, she said, and he wanted to take her to Paris for the weekend. Corinne had made an excuse, but she said she might go if he asked her again.

The dress had been worth the money, she said. He'd taken her to an expensive restaurant and told her that she looked beautiful. He had a nice car and a flat of his own in nearby Weybridge; he worked for his family's property company.

Kerry saw a flicker of wistfulness pass over Zoey's face. She remembered what she'd said about missing the excitement of getting to know somebody new. A glance at her watch told her it was just twenty past five, forty minutes to go before Jake finished his spot and she'd be able to talk to him.

She leaned forward, cupped her chin in her hands, and made a determined effort to join in.

Jake finished his spot five minutes early, when the saxophonist arrived to do the next one. Quickly, he put his guitar in its case, then raced over to Kerry's table.

"Hey," the saxophonist said, "you haven't emptied the box."

"I'll do it later," Jake said.

The saxophonist emptied the money box himself, and put the money aside for Jake.

Kerry saw him coming, and smiled. He was grinning so broadly, she was sure he'd got the contract; he wouldn't look like that if he'd had bad news. Inside her chest, her heart was beating like a drum.

Calm down, she told herself. Take a deep breath.

"I got it," Jake said.

Kerry was so relieved, so pleased, that she couldn't say anything for a moment.

Jake sat down on the vacant chair.

"Got what?" Corinne said, casually. She'd spent the whole time talking about her date and considering whether she should change the colour of her nail polish.

Jake hardly noticed her. "The recording contract," he said, looking directly at Kerry. "I'm doing a single that they're going to release in the autumn.

If that goes well, they want me to do an album. So I'm on my way, at last."

Zoey laughed. It hadn't taken Jake so long, but then he was very talented.

Kerry's voice was weak, like she had a cold coming on. "I'm thrilled, Jake," she said. "But I knew you'd get it. This one or the next one. I was pretty sure."

"Huh? I wasn't. I've hardly slept all week. Every time the phone rang, I jumped. I wouldn't like to go through that again."

"You won't have to," Kerry croaked, coughing to ease the dryness in her throat. Talking to Jake, being close to him, always made her feel faint. For a moment or two, she and Jake just gazed at each other, then she realized that he didn't have a drink, and that he'd need one after all that singing.

"Can I get you a coffee?" she asked him.

"A Coke, but it's my treat."

Kerry stood up. "No," she said, "it's mine. To celebrate."

Jake laughed. When she came back with the Coke and more coffees, they drank to his future.

Jake's deep blue eyes were constantly on Kerry. He hardly looked away from her once, and although she adored his interest, it made her feel terribly shy. She didn't want to say anything, to do anything to break the mood.

"I'm recording the single next week," he said. "I was hoping you'd come with me."

Kerry took a breath. She'd get the time off, she'd *have* to get the time off. The editor had said, last time, it wasn't as if Jake had a recording contract, but now he did. She'd beg, plead, beseech, nag. If she had to, she'd quit the job.

"We'd *love* to come," Corinne said, smiling, her eyes twinkling.

Zoey gasped and glared at her.

Kerry felt as if she'd been punched in the stomach.

Jake was looking at *her*, ignoring Corinne.

"I'd ... I'd really like to come, Jake," Kerry said. She had been going to say, "I'd love to come," but she didn't want to mimic Corinne.

Corinne, who was sitting besides her, linked her arm through Kerry's. "Yes," she said, "it'll be brill!"

Jake's eyes flickered over her, then back to Kerry. "Great," he said. "It's on Friday. We'll get the eight a.m. train to London."

He finished his Coke and got up. "Have to go," he said. "I've got dishes to wash."

Zoey laughed. Kerry just gazed at him. Corinne was sitting there, looking like a cat drunk on cream.

Jake left.

Zoey nudged Kerry. "Go after him," she hissed.

Kerry hesitated.

"*Go on!*"

Kerry caught up with Jake at the door of the mall.

"I'm really pleased about the contract," she said, nervously. "I ... I didn't sleep much either."

He grinned, and she had to suppress an urge to throw her arms around him and hug him tight.

"I'm sorry about Corinne."

Jake shrugged. "It doesn't matter."

Kerry's heart leapt; if he *was* interested in Corinne he wouldn't have said something like that. "I'm really looking forward to Friday," she said.

"So am I. I'm just, you know, trying to keep my feet on the ground. I won't get the money for a while, so I'm keeping my jobs. I..." He stopped talking for a moment.

"Yes?" Kerry said, hopefully.

"The song, the single, I've only just written it. I've got to work on it, you know, do the arrangements for the backing and so on. So I won't have much time. But after the recording..."

His voice tailed off again. He *is* shy, Kerry thought.

"Maybe," Jake said, slowly, "maybe we can spend some time together then."

"That would be nice," Kerry said.

He smiled, and, once again, she wanted to hug him.

"See you," he said.

When she got back to Zoey and Corinne, Zoey had an angry expression on her face. Corinne looked the picture of injured innocence.

"It's not Jake," she said, when Kerry sat down. "I just want to go because we might meet someone *really* famous. You know, a real pop star. I mean, as far as you and Jake are concerned, I won't even be there."

"Yes," said Zoey, "but three's a crowd."

"Oh, grow up, Zoey," Corinne said. "Kerry doesn't mind. Do you, Kerry?"

They were both looking at her.

"I'd rather I was going alone with Jake," Kerry said.

"Oh, *come on*. It's not as if you're going out on a date. You're going to a recording studio, and there'll be dozens of other people around."

Kerry said nothing.

"He'll be playing most of the time. I'll be able to keep you company," Corinne said.

"Sure," Kerry said.

6

On Saturday morning, Kerry turned her entire wardrobe out. There was nothing in it that would do, nothing that she hadn't worn dozens of times before. She wanted to look good, to look special for Jake. The people in the recording studio would be blasé, streetwise; she didn't want to look like some hick from the suburbs.

There was a couple of weeks' wages in her cash-card account, there had been more but she'd spent quite a lot on the new CD-Rom that her little brother wanted for his birthday. Although she'd been touched by the look on his face when he opened the parcel, she almost regretted spending the money now.

Kerry withdrew most of the money and headed for the mall, her mother's words ringing in her ears: "If you're going to buy clothes, Kerry, get something that you'll get plenty of wear out of!"

Kerry winced at the image of the kind of clothes that her mother believed in, clothes that had never been in fashion and would never be, no matter how long she wore them for. When her father had seen the look on her face, he'd winked and told her to get whatever she wanted, she'd worked for the money, after all.

In the mall, she bypassed the branches of the chain stores and headed for the shop where she'd found her favourite top. There, she tried on some dresses and trousers mixed with different tops, but she didn't find anything that really jumped out at her. She wanted so much to find something really special, something that would help her to look as good as she could.

It was the same in the other shops. It was nearly sale time, all the best things had gone.

She walked along the mall, stopping at the designer boutique where Corinne bought most of her clothes. Diffidently, she pushed the door open and walked inside; she'd never been in before. The shop was quiet, after the bustle of the mall; music played softly in the background, and the assistants smiled at her. Kerry was the only customer; shyly, she began to browse.

The rails were full of famous names, Ralph Lauren and Armani jeans.

Clothes to die for, Kerry thought, as she flicked through them. The Versace dresses were hundreds of pounds, even the T-shirts cost forty or fifty. Her heart sank. At the end of the rail, though, she found a little red silk dress that she could afford, although it would cost all of the money she had.

Kerry tried the dress on. It fitted her perfectly, made her feel sleek and sophisticated. She walked out of the fitting room to look at herself in the big mirror. The perfect cut flattered her figure.

"That dress could've been made for you," the assistant said.

Kerry smiled. She thought so too.

She turned this way and that, the flared skirt moved perfectly; it wasn't too short, but just right for her height.

"Of course," the assistant said, "you'd need a pair of strappy sandals. We have the perfect ones. Would you like to try them?"

Kerry gulped. She had not thought of shoes, but now that she did, she realized that her black clogs wouldn't do, nor would the lace-ups she wore to work. The only sandals she had were last year's, and they were badly scuffed.

"How ... how much are they?"

"I'm not sure," the assistant said. "I'll have a look to see."

She came back with a pair of wonderfully strappy black sandals.

Kerry gasped when she saw the price, she wondered if she could get anything cheaper somewhere else, but if she paid for the dress, she'd have nothing left. And the dress on its own was useless.

The assistant leaned towards her. "If you wait a couple of weeks it'll be half price in the sale," she said, "the sandals as well."

Kerry laughed. "I'll come back," she said, as she went to take the dress off.

Corinne came in then. She grinned at Kerry, whistled at the dress. "Are you going to take it?" she asked her.

Kerry was still smarting from her muscling in on her day out with Jake. "I'm not sure," she said, trying to feign nonchalance.

In the changing booth, she noticed that her face had gone red. She took the dress off and handed it to the assistant, then left quickly while Corinne was engrossed in a rack of lycra.

What do I do now? Kerry wondered, as she wandered back through the mall towards the High Street. A couple of weeks ago, she'd seen an outfit in one of the Sunday papers, a pair of slim trousers with a matching jacket that the paper said was the hottest style for the summer. The department store that sold it didn't have a branch in Alton, so Kerry took the bus to Kingston.

There, she discovered that the suit was sold out, not only in Kingston but nationwide. Kerry walked back to the bus-stop, past the branches of the chain stores where everything looked the same to her.

What now? she wondered, as she passed the Oxfam Shop. Something caught her eye, she wasn't sure what – she had to look again before she saw the black denim and leather matching jeans and jacket in the window.

Kerry blinked and saw the designer label, looked again because she didn't believe her eyes.

She pushed the door open and went into the shop, sniffing the scent of old clothes and lavender. "The suit in the window, can I try it on?" she asked.

One of the helpers fetched it for her. "It's £9.99, dear, is that all right?" she asked, as she handed it to her.

"It's fine," Kerry mumbled, unable to believe her luck.

The jeans and jacket fitted as if they'd been made for her. Kerry bought it, giving Oxfam an extra £5 in gratitude, then she went and bought a plain white T-shirt to go with it and a pair of canvas mules and a matching canvas shoulder bag.

When she got home, she tried it all on. The clothes looked perfect, just right for a recording studio, and all for less than £40.

Kerry pinched herself, still unable to believe her good luck.

Time began to pass very slowly again. On Wednesday afternoon, Kerry thought, It's not too bad, I'll see him again in a couple of hours. She'd taken the outfit to the dry-cleaner's, to make sure that it would be pristine.

Her phone rang just before she left the office.

"Hi," Jake said.

Kerry felt butterflies fluttering around in her stomach.

"Hi," she said, suddenly afraid that he was calling to cancel Friday.

"I just thought I'd phone to tell you that I won't be at the mall today," he said.

"Oh?" she replied, trying to keep the disappointment out of her voice.

"I'm working on the song I'm recording on Friday, so Keith's doing my spot."

"Keith?"

"The saxophonist. Can you still make it on Friday?"

"Yes," Kerry said. "I'm looking forward to it."

"See you then," he said, putting the phone down.

Kerry called up the calculator on the computer, worked out that she'd see him again in forty hours and forty minutes. That didn't sound so terrible. But forty hours and forty minutes was a total of two thousand, four hundred and forty minutes. Kerry tapped in 6 and 0, then hit the multiplier button.

One hundred and forty-six thousand, four hundred seconds.

Kerry winced, and wondered if she could wait that long.

On Friday morning, Kerry got up at six. She showered and washed her hair, then partly dryed it with the dryer, leaving it to finish drying naturally, because it looked best that way. Once she'd put her new T-shirt on, she put a little make-up on, just a touch of kohl and lip- and eye-gloss, then she dabbed the CK One that she'd got as a free sample behind her ears and on the base of the throat. The sachet of perfume had been in her drawer for ages; she'd been keeping it for a special occasion.

Finally, she put the Gaultier jacket on, then she picked up the bag and studied her reflection in the mirror.

She didn't need Zoey to tell her that she was looking really good.

Kerry was too nervous for breakfast. Last night, she'd put new batteries in her tape recorder and checked them; she checked them again, then put her reporter's notebook and several pens in her bag. It wouldn't do to miss the big quote. After making sure that she had her purse and her cash card, she left the house at seven, unable to wait any longer. If she took the long way to the station, that would use up half an hour.

Kerry saw Jake as soon as she walked into the booking office. She noticed that he flushed when he saw her.

"I've got your ticket," he said.

"Thanks, but you didn't have to. The editor wants me to do a story, so the paper will pay."

Jake shrugged. "It doesn't matter."

It was still only twenty past seven.

Jake looked around, asked her if she wanted a coffee. They went into the smoky cafeteria, where businessmen were reading the morning papers. Kerry insisted on buying the coffees, because Jake had paid for her ticket. She noticed that her hands were shaky when she picked up the tray to carry it to the table.

Jake's hands were trembling too. As he picked up his coffee, a little spilled on the table.

"Oops," he said, grinning shyly.

Kerry mopped the spilt coffee up with a paper napkin. "It's not every day you record your first single."

He laughed as he held his hands out so that she could see them shake. "I can't believe it," he said. "I've been up all night, going over the arrangements. I keep on thinking that I've written the wrong note down somewhere."

"I'm sure you haven't."

"I know, but I have to check, you know?"

Kerry did. Gingerly, she picked up her own coffee and took a sip. It was very hot, scalding her tongue. As she put the cup down, a little spilled out on to her T-shirt.

"Whoops," she said. "Me too."

Jake grinned at her. "That makes me feel a little better."

She got up. "I'll just go and wash it out."

"If it leaves a stain," Jake said, "turn it around and wear it back to front. That's what my sister does."

When Kerry came back, her coffee had cooled down and she managed to drink it. Jake began to tell her about the musicians he'd be playing with; he'd met most of them when he made the demo but he needed a pianist on the single, so he said he might record the track himself, and get the engineers to mix it in to the master tape. Kerry didn't understand the jargon, she had to keep on interrupting to ask him what he meant. Jake explained it all to her patiently; he didn't mind, he said, he'd rather she asked questions than got confused. He told her that once he got into the studio, he'd probably be totally absorbed in the music, but that didn't mean that he was ignoring her, or he wasn't glad that she was there. It was just that when he started to play, time had a way of coming to a halt; he often did not realize how much time had passed until he looked at his watch.

Jake talked expressively with his hands, and

Kerry found herself watching them, wondering what it would feel like to be holding one of them. Inwardly, she shivered, then she smiled.

"What is it?" Jake asked her.

"Oh, nothing," Kerry said, looking down at her empty coffee cup.

He reached out with one finger and drew her chin up so that she faced him. "Tell me..." he said. "Tell me what you were smiling about."

Kerry blushed and felt a thrill because it was the first time he had touched her.

They were staring into each other's eyes; the busy sounds of the café faded and they were alone with themselves. Kerry found herself wishing that they didn't have to get on the train and go to London, or do anything else, just that this moment could last for ever.

"Hi," Corinne said.

Startled, Jake looked up at Kerry's friend. Kerry groaned, then she forced herself to smile too.

"We have a date, remember?" Corinne said brightly, her long blonde hair swinging as she sat down besides Jake.

Kerry gulped. Corinne was wearing a red dress, *the* red dress that she'd tried on herself, but couldn't afford. She also had the little strappy sandals, and a matching bag. She looked terrific.

"I like your dress," Kerry said, carefully.

"It looked so good on you," Corinne said. "I couldn't resist it. I hope you don't mind."

Kerry smiled. "Of course not."

Corinne cast her eyes over Kerry's outfit. "Gaultier," she said, knowingly.

Kerry nodded.

"Last year's," Corinne said.

Kerry said nothing as Corinne turned to Jake and asked him what famous pop stars she'd meet at the studio.

Kerry opened her mouth to say "Jake Michaels", but she closed it before any sound came out.

Jake smiled politely. "Most of the really big ones have their own studios," he said, "but the backing guys have worked with most of the big names."

"Such as?"

"Just about everybody who's ever had a hit record."

Corinne looked disappointed.

They got on to the train, squeezing into a carriage full of commuting secretaries and junior managers. Corinne had her own ticket: Kerry was relieved that Jake had not bought one for her as well.

Jake looked a little uncomfortable as Corinne prattled on about this and that. Kerry looked at her and wondered what her friend was playing at.

That was, if Corinne really was her friend.

Half-way, to London, Corinne looked her up and down.

"Your T-shirt's on back to front," she said.

The recording studio was in St John's Wood, an area of wide avenues, leafy trees, and gracious white Georgian houses.

Kerry felt a thrill when she saw a plaque on the wall which said that The Beatles' *Abbey Road* had been recorded in this very studio. There were also dozens of gold and platinum discs, of all sorts of groups and singers from Take That to Luciano Pavarotti.

Beside her, she felt Jake stiffen with nerves. Corinne acted as if she owned the place.

Jake cleared his throat and gave his name to the receptionist, who looked good enough to be on the cover of *Vogue*.

"Oh, you're Jake Michaels," she said. "I *love* your demo."

Jake grinned shyly.

"You're in studio one," the receptionist said, leading the way on willowy legs. She was wearing hot pants that looked as if they had been painted on. "They've been practising the backing."

Jake nodded to himself.

When they reached the door of the studio, the receptionist offered them drinks. Jake shook his head; he wanted to start work. He went straight into the studio, telling Kerry and Corinne that he would see them later. The receptionist showed them into a small room next to the control room where they could watch what was going on.

"Just dial 0 on the phone if you want anything," she said. "Help yourself to coffee and drinks from the fridge."

Kerry sat down, but she sank into the soft cushions of the chair and she couldn't see through the window, so she got up and stood to watch.

Jake had taken his guitar out of the case and was checking the tuning. Apart from him, there was a man playing the bass guitar, another on keyboards and a drummer. After Jake had finished tuning, they talked together in a huddle. Kerry couldn't hear what they were saying, so she turned the knob next to the window. Jake's amplified voice boomed into the room, so loud that she jumped.

Kerry adjusted the sound and settled down to watch and listen. Jake was talking to the pianist, explaining to him how he wanted the track played. The pianist ran through it once, then Jake played it himself to show him how he wanted it. Meanwhile the bass guitar player was strumming to himself.

Kerry thought there was something familiar about the tune, although she didn't recognize it.

"Wow," Corinne said, behind her. "There's caviare in the fridge, and champagne."

Kerry turned around and saw that she was about to help herself. "Don't," she said, quickly.

"Why not?"

"It's Jake's session. We're only here as a privilege."

"She said to help ourselves," Corinne said, pouting, although she left the champagne, taking an orange juice instead.

Kerry turned back to Jake and the musicians. After he'd worked on the piano track for a while, he said, "Right, let's go for a run through."

Jake began to play his guitar, then the others joined in. As Jake began to sing, Kerry realized with a thrill that they were recording the song that she loved, *The Girl With The Smile In Her Eyes*.

They finished the song.

A voice boomed out from the control room. "That sounded good. Do you want play-back?"

"Let's try it one more time," Jake said. "The phrasing was a little loose." He said something to the bass guitarist, then they played the track again. This time, Jake listened as the track was played back through the speakers.

There was a frown on his face as the last note died. "It's still a bit loose," he said. "I know it's a ballad, but I want it clean and sharp."

Kerry was amazed and delighted. She couldn't believe that what she'd just heard was the same song that Jake had played in the mall. It sounded so real, so professional; just as good, even better than, the songs she listened to on the radio.

Jake listened as, one by one, the musicians played their tracks individually. Then they recorded the song several times without any lyrics.

"I'm bored," Corinne said, during a lull between recordings.

"Ssshh," hissed Kerry.

Corinne looked at her watch. "It's after twelve. They've been at it for *ages*."

Just then the receptionist came in and asked them if they'd like salads for lunch, or if they wanted to order something in.

"What's Jake having?" Kerry asked her.

"I haven't asked him yet, but last time he had a tandoori."

Kerry said she'd have whatever Jake was having; Corinne asked for a chicken salad.

"You're so unassertive," she said, when the receptionist left.

Kerry looked down at her fingernails. "I just don't want to cause any problems for Jake," she said.

Jake was now singing the words of *The Girl With The Smile In Her Eyes* to the backing track he'd already recorded. When he finished and it was played back, he winced and said he thought he was going just a little off-key in the chorus. The voice from the control room said they'd take a break for lunch, and Corinne sighed with relief.

They had lunch in the patio behind the studio, sitting on wicker seats underneath an oak tree. The sun was summer-bright, almost blinding in its intensity.

"How did it go?" Kerry asked Jake.

He looked at her. "You heard."

"It sounded good to me."

He shook his head. "It's not there yet. But it's close. Maybe another couple of takes will do it."

He ate quickly, anxiously, as if he was oblivious to the food and just wanted to get on with the recording. Suddenly, he looked embarrassed. "You're not bored, are you, Kerry?"

"Bored? No, I'm fascinated." Kerry's notebook was already half-full; she'd carefully noted every detail of the studio, from the recording and playback equipment to the contents of the fridge.

Jake grinned shyly. "That's good. If the single goes well, I'll be spending a lot of time in the studio over the next year."

"What about college?"

He shrugged. "I don't know, yet. I'd like to finish my degree, but it's a practical course, I can take a break if I need to. Thing is, in this business, you've got to grab your chances while you can."

Kerry nodded. She noticed that Corinne was paying rapt attention to one of the recording engineers, who was telling her stories about the singer whose album was No. 1 in the charts.

After lunch, she went into the control room with him while Kerry sat watching Jake sing *The Girl With The Smile In Her Eyes* time and time again. Finally, he asked for play-back.

Kerry was so engrossed that she didn't notice that a man had come into the room to listen with her.

He cleared his throat and she jumped.

"Hi," he said. "I'm Tim Sloan from Reflex Records. You must be Jake's girlfriend?"

Kerry blushed. "I'm just a friend," she said. "I'm doing a story about the recording for the *Alton Gazette*."

Tim Sloan nodded as he listened to the music. Kerry noticed that his foot was tapping in time with the beat. She thought that was a good sign. He seemed quite young, but the clothes that he wore looked very expensive and there was an aura of power around him.

Kerry held her breath until the recording finished. Jake asked for it to be played again.

Tim Sloan was smiling to himself. When the music finished, he moved to the window and pressed a button.

"Sounds good, Jake."

Jake grinned broadly. "You don't think it's a little raw?"

"I think it's perfect, Jake. I think that's the master."

Jake turned to thank the musicians.

Tim Sloan turned to Kerry. "What d'you think?"

"I think it's great," she said, "but then I'm biased."

He grinned. "Would you buy it?"

"If I didn't know Jake, maybe," Kerry said. "But what I'd do most likely would be to tape it off the radio."

Tim Sloan laughed. "At least you're honest. I think Jake's really got something. It'll go down well with the late-teen market and the twenties as well. It's a good pop song, but it's also got depth. It's a catchy tune, the sort of thing that sticks in your mind. The lyrics are thoughtful. I really like it. That's why I bought it."

Kerry smiled politely. She really didn't know what to say to this man who held Jake's future in the palm of his hand.

Jake came out of the studio. He looked exhausted, ready to drop. One of the engineers asked him how many tapes he wanted. He asked for two, and one for Kerry.

Tim Sloan looked at his watch, then he asked them if they'd like to go out for dinner. Kerry looked at Jake, who blushed deeply.

"Uh, I've got this job washing dishes in the evening," he said. "I haven't quit yet and, well, they've been good to me, I don't like to leave them in the lurch."

Tim Sloan grinned. "It's good that you've got a sense of decency, Jake. Some other time, yes?"

"Sure," Jake said.

Before he left, Tim Sloan ordered a car to take them all back to Alton. Corinne came out of the control room, having made a date with the recording engineer.

"He says Jake's *really* good," she said to Kerry, as Jake was picking up his tapes. "He says he's going to make it, he'll be the next big star."

Kerry shrugged. She knew that already.

When the car came, it was a limo, complete with TV and hi-fi, cocktail cabinet, fax and phone.

Kerry gasped.

The chauffeur held the door open for them. Kerry got in first, then Corinne sat beside her. Jake took the seat opposite them. Corinne jumped up and then sat down beside him. "If you're going to be a superstar, you shouldn't be alone," she said.

Kerry felt a stab of jealousy; Jake looked embarrassed.

Before he drove off, the chauffeur offered them drinks. Jake had a beer, Corinne asked for champagne. Kerry had a diet Coke.

Kerry looked at Jake. "How're you feeling?"

"Washed out. I can't believe I actually did it. I keep on expecting to wake up and find that it's a dream."

She smiled. "I promise you, it isn't."

The streets of London passed smoothly. The inside of the limo was like a mobile living-room.

"This is brill," Corinne said. "I just hope someone I know sees me." She began to talk about rock stars, telling Jake some of the stories the recording engineer had told her. Kerry could see that Jake was bored. She looked at Corinne and hated her for a moment, just for being there.

I mean, she thought, as she watched her chatter on, you don't even like him, or you say you don't. So why d'you have to butt in like this?

Jake was the only boy she liked, this was the first date she'd had since she came to Alton. Even though it wasn't a proper date, every moment was precious and just by being there, Corinne was ruining it. In the last few weeks, Corinne had had several dates, and she'd turned down at least one other one.

It wasn't as if she was short of chances.

Kerry leaned back and remembered what Zoey had said: Corinne's father made everything so easy for her that she didn't really value anything she had, because she never had to struggle and work the way most people do. That included boys.

Right then, Corinne was flirting with Jake, tossing her head back like a horse and fixing him with these big blue eyes of hers. Jake wasn't saying much; Kerry sensed he was embarrassed, but Corinne ignored that because his feelings didn't matter, only her own did. She didn't like Jake at all for what he was, only because of what he might become.

A wave of anger swept over Kerry, she bit her lip and gripped the seat tightly, afraid that Jake's feelings for her – whatever feelings he had because she wasn't sure yet – might be shaded by assumptions he'd make about the girl who was, had been, her friend.

Corinne was talking about the music business as if she was an expert, but all she knew was what she'd picked up that day.

"D'you like live concerts?" she asked Jake.

"Sure."

"Who's your favourite?"

"I don't get to many, it's too expensive."

Kerry felt a lump form inside her stomach. She shot a vicious look at Corinne, but Corinne's attention was fixed on Jake.

"I've got tickets for the Music Channel Party," Corinne said. "Everybody'll be there. Apparently, Elton John's doing a spot, and there's all the bands from the charts."

Kerry blinked. She'd had the tickets, she should've thought to ask him if he'd like to go. But that was before he'd asked her to the recording, and she hadn't wanted him to think that she was crowding him, and most of all, she'd been afraid that he would turn her down.

"Why don't you come along?" Corinne said.

Kerry looked at her as she felt ice form in her heart.

"Uh, I don't know," Jake said. "It's kind of you, but..."

"You're not working on Sunday, are you?"

"No, but..."

"Well, come then," Corinne said.

"Uh, OK," Jake said.

Kerry looked away, out through the tinted windows, hoping that neither of them would see the tears in her eyes.

7

Kerry faced Corinne. "How could you?" she asked her.

It was Saturday morning; they were in the mall with Zoey. They'd arranged to meet up before the recording, but Kerry didn't think that Corinne would have the neck to turn up. But she had. Worse, she was flashing her credit card, saying that she only had time for a quick cappuccino before she hit the summer sales. She'd breezed in as Kerry was finishing telling Zoey the story, as if nothing had happened and she had done nothing wrong.

"Yes," Zoey said. "How could you, Corinne?"

Corinne looked at each of them in turn. A flicker passed over her face before she spoke. "I don't know what you're talking about," she said. "He said he liked concerts, and I had tickets. So I asked him to come. So what?"

Zoey looked up to the heavens. "Corinne," she said, slowly. "They were Kerry's tickets..."

"She gave them to me."

"I know, but you could've given them back to her, let her go with Jake. You know how much he means to her."

Corinne shrugged. "It's no big deal."

Zoey sighed. "Corinne, come on. It's the hottest ticket in town!"

Corinne looked hurt. "Kerry had her chance to ask him and she didn't. I did. So what? Besides, you know what they say. All's fair in love and war. Kerry had her chance, and she blew it."

Kerry got up and walked away. Zoey followed her.

"Kerry," she said, "don't let her get to you."

"How can I not let her get to me when she does something like that?"

Zoey pursed her lips. "That's just Corinne. She's so spoiled, everything she wants she gets. Jake's just something else that she wants. She'll change her mind about him tomorrow or the next day, as soon as she meets someone else."

It hurt Kerry so much to hear Zoey talking about Jake like that. She said nothing.

"Somehow, I don't think that Jake's the kind of boy who'd fall for Corinne," Zoey said.

Kerry struggled to smile, but she couldn't quite manage it.

"Maybe Corinne's right," she said, bitterly. "I had my chance, and I blew it."

"I don't think so. I still think Jake's shy. He'll be really put off by someone like her."

Kerry thought again about what Jake had said to Corinne. *Well, I don't know. But... But... OK.*

That final OK was enough.

"I should have known," she said. "I should have asked him myself."

"Kerry, don't be like that. Jake really likes you. I know he does. He'll come back to you, I'm sure he will. Just wait and see."

"But Corinne's so ... so..."

"So what?" Zoey asked.

"So sophisticated, I suppose. It's all so easy for her."

Zoey shook her head. "She's spoilt, and she's a flirt. But underneath it all, she's not totally bad. I bet she's feeling rotten, despite what she said. There was a funny look on her face."

Kerry left the mall. She didn't want to talk about it any more. She just wished that Corinne would drop dead.

When she got home, she went up to her room and threw herself down on the bed. Her parents were away sailing with her little brother, she had the house all to herself. But there was nothing she wanted to do, nothing that could get her the chance of Jake back again. She was convinced that she'd lost him to Corinne, and she could not bear the pain of it.

Kerry dozed through the afternoon, dreaming if-onlys.

The phone rang at half past five. For a long time, she lay there, wondering whether she should answer it or not. In her dreams, it was Jake calling, to tell her that he wasn't going to the Music Channel Party with Corinne, that if he couldn't go with her, he wouldn't go with anyone.

Kerry dreamed on for a moment, then she got up tiredly to answer the phone. She was being silly, she told herself. The caller wasn't Jake, it would be someone for her parents, or maybe her brother.

Just as she got to the phone, the ringing stopped.

Too bad, she told herself. If it was Jake, it would serve him right that she hadn't answered it.

Although most of her anger was directed at Corinne, she was also angry with him.

The phone rang again at five to eight, when Kerry was having a long, hot bath. She had taken a pizza out of the freezer, and was planning to eat it while she watched a video. Kerry got out of the bath, but the phone stopped ringing the moment she picked it up.

Too bad, she told herself again.

Jake put the phone down. He'd spent the day ringing all the Smiths in the phone book. He'd rung hundreds of numbers and narrowed the hunt down to fifteen, who hadn't answered. One of these numbers was bound to be Kerry's, and he'd carefully noted the addresses of all of them.

It had been a long day, and Jake was getting sick of the sound of his own voice, saying: "Please, can I speak to Kerry?" and then apologizing when the person who answered told him that there was no Kerry there.

He could start the hunt again tomorrow. Right now, he had things to do, dishes to wash.

Kerry had told the chauffeur to stop at the station when he'd asked who wanted to be dropped off first. As soon as the car drew to a halt, she took off at a run.

Shaken, Jake had gone out of the limo after her, but she'd run straight across the road and when he tried to follow her a car came along.

"Kerry!" he yelled, but she didn't listen, or maybe she didn't hear him because she was already too far away. When there was a pause in the traffic, Jake ran after her but when he turned the corner at the end of the station road she had gone.

Jake stopped then, realizing that it was futile to run after her any longer, also that he'd left his precious guitar in the boot of the limo. Slowly, he walked back to the limo, got in and sat down after he'd given the driver his own address.

Corinne had opened another half-bottle of champagne.

Jake began to ask her for Kerry's address, then, when he saw the look on her face, he stopped.

The chauffeur dropped her off first.

"See you on Sunday," she said. "The bus leaves the mall at half past five."

"Er, no," Jake said. "I've just remembered, I'm doing something else."

An angry look spread over Corinne's pretty features, making her look plain, almost ugly, for a moment.

She slammed the door so hard that the limo shook.

That night, as Jake washed dishes in the *trattoria* in silence, he did not hum at all as he usually did.

* * *

He slept late on Sunday morning. At first, when he went to bed, he hadn't been able to sleep at all, because he was thinking about Kerry. His thoughts drifted all night, over how hurt she'd looked, how he'd never meant to hurt her, had never even dreamt of it. When Corinne had mentioned the concert, it had been no big deal to him, the kind of thing that went on all the time at college, people sharing tickets to things because good tickets were always hard to come by. It was only when he saw the look on Kerry's face that he realized she was upset.

He cursed himself then, but he'd already agreed to go, and just after that Kerry had fled.

When he got up, aching and still tired, just after ten, his sister Merry was on the phone to her boyfriend. Jake was so busy that he hadn't seen much of her, but he knew it was a serious relationship and he'd heard her saying something about having to sort some problem out.

Merry talked for more than an hour, and when she'd finished and Jake went to begin his calls, she put her hand over the phone and begged him to wait a while, because she was waiting for her boyfriend to call her back.

"I won't be long," Jake said.

"*Please*," Merry begged. "It's *so* important. After he calls, you can have the phone all to yourself."

Jake waited for an hour, then he went out and got some change at the newsagent's to make the calls from the coinbox just along the road. He spent most of the afternoon there; the booth was busy because it was near the swimming pool and people kept on wanting to call a cab and things like that.

By the time Jake finished, he'd narrowed the hunt down to three numbers that hadn't answered. As he walked back home, he thought that the addresses were all quite close, he could easily walk to them all. Then he realized that there was little point; if the people weren't answering their phone, they weren't likely to be in.

Jake went into his studio instead, and began to work on a song he'd been thinking about. Again, it was about Kerry, but this time it was about the way she'd been when he was waiting to hear about the recording contract. He remembered the way she'd said, "I'll keep my fingers crossed," and wondered if he could work the lyrics around that, or if the line was too much of a cliché.

He began to strum some chords. Soon, he was absorbed in his music.

8

Kerry finished the story on Jake's recording session, then she pressed the key to send it to the editor. He'd asked her for it as soon as she came in on Monday morning, because he wanted to run it in the colour feature pages that week, and the pages went to bed before the news section. He was using a close-up from the pictures of Jake that had been taken in the mall.

Although Kerry tried hard, the words just would not come. She'd worked on the story all morning and through her lunch hour; as she sent it off to the editor, she knew that it wasn't good, but it was the best that she could do.

The careful notes she'd taken blurred when she looked at them; she'd been so happy then, so full of hope. Now, she was struggling to come to terms with the knowledge that Jake didn't like her as much as she had thought he'd done; he simply couldn't, because if he had, he'd never have agreed to go to the Music Channel Party with Corinne.

She read the piece over again, wincing at the memory. It wasn't too bad, she thought, it just wasn't as good as she could do, as she had done last time.

The sub-editor read the story first to check it before the editor looked at it. As soon as he finished, he called over to Kerry and asked her what the title of Jake's first single was.

"Uh, I think it's *The Girl With The Smile In Her Eyes*," Kerry said.

"You better call him and make sure," the sub said.

Kerry picked up the phone. "I'll call the record company," she said.

The PR manager at Reflex Records said that *The Girl With The Smile In Her Eyes* was only the working title, they hadn't decided what the final title would be, so Kerry made a small change in her story and sent it back to the editor.

Then she waited for his reaction, a little afraid that he'd pick up the hurt she'd felt as she had written it.

When her phone rang, she picked it up quickly, thinking that it would be the editor.

"Hi," Corinne said. "Where have you been? I called you hundreds of times yesterday."

"I was out," Kerry said, dully. She'd gone out with her parents and her brother for a picnic and then they'd gone to a movie, so they hadn't been back till late, but she didn't want to tell Corinne that she'd been with her family.

"Oh?" Corinne said, waiting for an explanation, but Kerry did not give her one.

"The reason I called," she went on, "is that I decided not go with Jake."

"What?" Kerry said.

"Yup. I thought, what a bum, I mean, making a date with your girlfriend's girlfriend. Who'd want to go out with a guy like that?"

I do, Kerry thought. "I was never his girlfriend," she said.

"I just wanted to tell you before anyone else did," Corinne said. "I ended up going with my brother, but we had an absolutely brill time. It was mega!"

"Great," Kerry said, dully.

"In any case," Corinne said, "I'm really sorry. I didn't realize that you were upset until I saw you take off like that. I just said that you were one of my best friends, my best friend of all, really, and I didn't want to do anything to hurt you."

"Oh," said Kerry, feeling a pain in the pit of her stomach. If anything, things were worse. Now Jake knew from Corinne how she felt about him.

"He's just a jerk." Corinne said. "I wouldn't bother about him, Kerry. I really wouldn't. There's plenty of other boys in Alton. Why don't you come to the country club on Saturday and I'll show you around?"

"Maybe," Kerry said. She looked up and saw the editor walking towards her, with a hard copy of her story in his hand.

"No hard feelings, right?" Corinne said. "Will you be at the mall later?"

"I guess so," Kerry said. "I have to go now. Bye."

The editor sat down in the chair by her desk.

"Kerry," he said, shaking his head. "This isn't up to your usual standard."

"What d'you mean?" she asked carefully.

"It's flat," he said. "There's no zing, no excitement. Here we have a local boy making his first single at the age of eighteen and you've reported it like it's a final of a club junior tennis match. Hey, he's about to hit the big time! Where's the colour? Where's the quotes?"

In my notebook, Kerry thought. "I'll go over it again."

"Good," the editor said, and then, when he saw the look on her face, "don't worry, every reporter has an off-day. That's what editors are for."

Carefully, methodically, Kerry began to work. She tried very hard, but no matter what she did, she could not make the story come alive. She worked until nearly six o'clock, when the editor told her to take a break, that he'd hold the story over for next week's edition.

"Don't worry," he said again. "It's just writer's block. It happens to everyone."

Kerry felt terrible when she left the newspaper office. Not only had she lost Jake, she'd also jeopardized her chance of the trainee's job. It was too late to go to the mall. She went home instead, and threw herself down on her bed, where she sobbed her heart out. She was angry with herself, annoyed that she'd been so unprofessional. Maybe I won't be able to be a reporter, she thought, maybe I'm just not good enough.

Later, she decided to try again. Working from her notes on her own computer, she stripped the story down to the bones, the facts, and then began to add her observations from her notebook, and also some quotes of Jake's and some from Tim Sloan. She wrote about the lavish hospitality of the recording studio, and the luxurious ride home in the limo. She finished with a jovial note that, after he'd finished the recording, Jake went off to wash dishes at the *trattoria*, as he always did on a Friday night.

Kerry breathed a sigh of relief. The story *was* good, she knew that. She knew that the editor would think so too, but it didn't matter. She hadn't managed to do it in time, and she'd missed the deadline.

She printed two copies of the story, then she went to bed, feeling pretty lousy about herself.

On Tuesday, she met Zoey at the mall for a sandwich at lunchtime. Kerry felt a little guilty, because she hadn't phoned, as she'd said she would. When Zoey rang her, she'd asked Kerry if she was avoiding her. The big news was that Julie was back from her holiday with Mike, her boyfriend. On their last night in Greece, Mike had asked her to marry him, and now she was wearing a silver engagement ring that they'd bought in the duty free shop at Corfu airport.

Kerry listened to Zoey as she told her all about it, feeling a pang of pain because now she knew that she'd never get to that stage with Jake.

Zoey was too diplomatic to ask about him. She knew from Kerry's expression that she hadn't heard from him. Once she finished telling Kerry all about

Julie, she started talking about how much money she'd managed to save from her supermarket wages, and how she was planning on keeping it until her 17th birthday, to pay for driving lessons.

After ten minutes of that, she'd run out of things to talk about.

Kerry cupped her chin in her hands. "Corinne said she didn't go to the Music Channel Party with Jake after all. She said she told him she'd changed her mind."

Zoey thought for minute.

"She said sorry," Kerry said.

"I should think so," Zoey said. "You know, last week, I didn't mean to defend her. I just meant, that's the way she is, and you just have to accept it or stop being friends with her. I really think, most of the time, she just jumps in. She doesn't realize what she's doing. It's her father, she's spoilt rotten."

"I don't know," Kerry said. "She seemed sincere on the phone, but she's so thoughtless."

"You don't say," Zoey said. "She went after Simon once."

"No!"

"Yes. It was at a party, and she asked him to dance, and she went on dancing with him for ages. I was absolutely mad, but after a long time Simon left her and came back to me. Corinne said she only did it because there was another boy there that she liked, and she thought she had a better chance with him if she danced with somebody else." She shrugged. "You see, I've known her all my life. I'm used to it. But every so often, I think that she's not my friend at all. Still, there's Julie. And now there's you."

Kerry smiled. She'd feel a lot worse if she didn't have Zoey.

"You'll come tomorrow?" Zoey asked her.

"You mean, when Jake's playing? I suppose so," Kerry said.

"Good," said Zoey. "Don't give up on him yet."

"I don't want to look like I'm chasing after him," Kerry said.

Zoey sighed. "We always met up in the afternoons before you met him," she said. "Why should we stop now?"

They paid the bill and then they went back to work. It was only later that Kerry realized that Zoey had seemed a little subdued.

Kerry went to the mall on Wednesday, as usual. Corinne was already there with Zoey, listening to Julie, who was rhapsodizing about the wedding she was planning in two years' time, as soon as Mike finished his college course. By then, she would have taken a secretarial course; she said that she didn't want a career, Mike was enough. Mike was studying computing; they were thinking of working abroad for a while before settling down.

"I think it's depressing," Corinne said, when Julie had finished. "You've got your whole life planned out, and you're only sixteen. Where's the excitement? Where's the thrill?"

Julie looked hurt. "We're not going to live together until we're married. That'll be a thrill.

We're going to travel together, see the world."

"What if you don't like living together once you're married?" Corinne asked her.

Julie sighed. "We've been together for three years, Corinne. It just gets better and better. We'd get married now except we can't afford to and my parents would go ape."

Corinne turned to Kerry. She handed her a carrier bag. "I nearly forgot. This is for you. It's to say that I'm sorry."

Kerry opened the bag and saw the red dress, the strappy sandals and the bag.

"I couldn't," she said.

"Don't be silly," Corinne said. "Dad just raised my allowance. I'll be really upset if you don't take it."

Suddenly, Kerry no longer wanted the dress. She handed it back to Corinne. "I don't want it," she said, "really. I changed my mind about red."

Corinne shrugged. "Suit yourself."

She had butterflies in her stomach, had felt them all afternoon in anticipation of seeing Jake, but as the time for his spot neared, the fluttering got worse. She could not drink her cappuccino, could hardly even swallow.

Zoey looked at her and winked. When Corinne started to talk about something else, she reached over and clasped Kerry's hand briefly.

Kerry glanced at her watch, saw the seconds tick by as the minute hand, torturously slowly, crept towards five o'clock. Ten to five passed, then five to; Jake was usually here by now. Where was he?

When five o'clock came the saxophonist who

usually followed Jake took his place and began to play.

Kerry felt nausea rise; Jake no longer cared about her, he didn't even care enough to tell her that he wouldn't be playing the spot at the mall.

Zoey saw the sad expression on her face. As they left, she linked her arm through Kerry's. "Come on," she said. "Let's go to my place. Everyone's away at Chris's degree show. We can have *spaghetti alla carbonara* and you can cry on my shoulder, if you want to."

Kerry smiled. "What would I do without you?"

Jake looked at the clock on the wall of the reception room. He was in the offices of Tony Steiger, one of the top managers in the music business. Steiger wasn't taking on new clients, he already had more than a dozen top acts, but he had agreed to see Jake on the strength of his demo tape and his contract with Reflex Records.

His secretary had told Jake to come at two o'clock, and she'd fit him in when she could. Just after three, she said it wouldn't be much longer, and Jake had called the saxophone player to ask him to do his spot at the mall. He'd also called Kerry at the paper, but she'd already left. Jake swore under his breath.

The thing was, he wasn't sure that he wanted or needed a manager, but his father had told him that it was important that he had good advice, and Jake thought that was sensible. He also knew that his father had a vested interest in his career, because he'd paid for his college course and lent him the money for the Stratocaster.

It was after five now, and, as far as Jake knew, Tony Steiger was still on a call from New York, the one that had come in nearly an hour before from Sony Music.

Jake waited, trying to be patient, wondering if he'd ever see Tony Steiger at all.

When he looked at the receptionist, she smiled brightly. "I'm sorry," she said, "it's just been one of these manic days. He'll see you as soon as he can. Would you like coffee, tea, a drink?"

Jake took a Coke, which he sipped slowly as he gazed at the wall full of pictures of bands, and gold and platinum discs. He was getting to know the music business now, how it liked to put its triumphs on display as if mega-success and super-stardom was all just a matter of course.

He'd never even thought about it, stardom. All he'd ever wanted was to make a record, to make more than one if he possibly could, to make a living out of playing songs that he wrote himself.

The distant possibility of stardom had never occurred to him. Now that it did, the thought sent a shiver down his spine. He did not know if he wanted that.

Correction: he wanted it, of course he did. He'd love to be able to play a venue like Wembley, to write the kind of songs that were played again and again until they became classics of their time.

He'd give his right arm to be able to write something like *Yesterday*.

But, then, he'd also give his right arm if he could wipe the hurt look from Kerry's face and make her smile again. He began to hum a tune, thought of the line *I'd do anything for you*, but somebody else had already written that.

Suddenly a door opened, and a small man strode towards him, holding his hand out for Jake to shake.

Jake stood up, dropping his tape and the song manuscript. He shook the offered hand, then bent down to pick them up, but Tony Steiger beat him to it.

"I'm really sorry I kept you waiting so long," he said. "But I've got a band touring America and it's just been one thing after another."

Jake smiled. Instantly, he decided he liked him; certainly, he wanted to listen to what he had to say.

Six hours later, Jake sat on the last train from Waterloo to Alton. He'd spent the evening with Tony, as the manager insisted he call him, first talking in his office, and then having dinner in a little Greek restaurant in Soho. He had to cancel his dishwashing, but Mario said it didn't matter, Wednesday was a slow day.

Tony had offered to take him on as a client, he said he loved his music and he thought he had a good future, but the single was just a beginning. He'd explained the process to him in fine detail, and Jake couldn't help being apprehensive.

As the train pulled out of the station, he closed his eyes and went over again what Tony had said.

"Y'see," he'd explained, "recording a single is just the first step on the way. There's tens of thousands of singles released every year, and most of them sink without trace. By that I mean they don't get enough airplay so they don't sell enough to make it viable for the record company, so the company drops the artiste. It happens all the time, and not just to the no-hopers, the flukes. It happens to some really good musicians. They have the talent, they have the songwriting ability, but somehow the single doesn't have the kind of charisma that it needs to sell. Sometimes it's just bad luck, sometimes the record company doesn't put enough muscle behind the release. Whatever, it is, it doesn't really matter, because once you've been dropped by one record company, it makes it that much harder to get another one to take you on.

"You've got to remember, Jake, record companies are in the business of selling records. Reflex aren't recording you because they like your music, they're doing it because they think they can sell enough of your single to make a profit. Sure, they know the statistics, that only about one in every few hundred new releases ever get anywhere, but they've decided that it's worth their while to give you a chance."

Jake had listened intently, his heart sinking. Numbly, he'd asked what his chances were.

Tony sat back, rocking his chair on its rear legs. "I'd say they were good, better than average. You're original, you've got your own sound. When you sent me your demo, I listened to it several times. We played it in the office and everybody liked it, you know, the secretaries were asking, who's that? If a major artiste recorded that number, I'm pretty sure it'd be a hit. But you're just starting out. The chances are, you won't make the charts."

"What can I do?" Jake asked. The way Tony was speaking, it was as if his record had already flopped.

The manager shrugged. "You haven't signed the contract yet?"

Jake shook his head.

"Well, you could pull out of the deal. If you haven't signed, it's not binding yet. I could book you in to some of the London clubs, and you could play that circuit for a while, maybe do a little television as well. Then you could put together material for an album and we could go back to Reflex or another company, and get a better deal. Thing is, because an album costs so much more, they'll put so much more muscle behind it."

Jake shook his head. "I wouldn't do that. I gave them my word. The single's already recorded."

Tony smiled. "I'm glad that's what you want to do. But I had to give you the option, that's my job as your manager. Don't worry about the marketing too much, just concentrate on your music. Reflex are a good company, and they like you a lot. I'm sure they'll be promoting you around the radio stations, and I know I will. But I did have to tell you about the downside, that's my job too. I wouldn't take you on if I didn't think you'd make it, if not with Reflex with somebody else. I just didn't want you to think that as soon as the single was released, you'd be on Top of the Pops. If it doesn't work this time, you just have to try again."

The train pulled into Alton Station. Jake got out

and began to walk home. On the way, he passed the street where Kerry lived. He'd found out her number at last, although when he'd rung a boy that must have been her brother told him that Kerry was out. Jake didn't leave a message; he didn't want to entrust something as important as his feelings for Kerry with anyone else.

He paused for a moment and then walked down the street and stood outside her house. He really wanted to talk to her, he needed to. Kerry, he was sure, could help him work out his doubts, find the courage to face the problems that would come when his record was released.

Tony had explained to him that whether it sold or not depended on the DJs on the big radio stations like Capital, Virgin Radio and, most of all, Radio 1, liking it enough to put it on the stations' play lists.

Jake's future now wasn't in the hands of Tim Sloan at Reflex Records, or even Tony. It was in the hands of a few DJs that he didn't know, couldn't even speak to for fear of being accused of hype.

Church bells began to chime, he counted to twelve. For a moment longer, he stood staring at Kerry's house, knowing that it was far too late to knock on her door.

There'd be other times to talk to her, to explain to her how vicious and frightening the music business was, to tell her how much it'd help if she was at his side.

Jake turned and walked away, thinking about her.

9

Friday was a slow day at the newspaper. The week's edition was published that day; all that happened was that the phones rang constantly with people asking about stories, and Kerry, as the most junior person in the office, had to take the calls.

She'd already put her story about Jake's recording session into the computer, and flagged it for the editor's attention. She was waiting anxiously for his reaction, but he'd spent the morning talking to people at Surrey Council about a new bypass, and then he'd gone off for lunch with the local MP.

When he came back, he looked distracted, so she didn't ask him about her story, although she was dying to hear what he thought. She felt terrible about Jake, but it seemed too cruel that because of her pain over him she'd lost the chance of the job that she really wanted.

Zoey had listened as she had gone over it again and again, and then hugged her as Kerry had sobbed her heart out. At first, Zoey had told her not to give up yet, but it had been a week now, and Jake hadn't rung yet.

Zoey kept on saying that Jake was shy, but it seemed to Kerry that he was also a little selfish.

Surely he knew that she liked him, that she'd be hurt when he didn't turn up at the mall to play his spot?

Three o'clock came. Kerry tidied up her desk, then went around the office, gathering up coffee cups to wash and emptying ashtrays. The only thing she didn't like about working on the paper was that most of the reporters smoked a lot. When she finished washing the cups, she put them back on the shelf in the little kitchen, then went back to her desk, to pick up her bag and her jacket.

The office was almost deserted. After the rush of the deadlines, most of the staff took the afternoon off. Kerry said goodbye to the picture editor, then went to the open door of the editor's office.

"Is there anything else?" she asked him nervously.

He looked up from the document he was reading, "No, Kerry. Thanks for your work. See you on Monday."

Kerry hesitated for a moment. "Did you get a chance to look at my story?"

He shook his head. "I don't have time now. I'll see it on Monday."

Kerry felt disappointment sweep over her. She left the office and headed for the mall. "Damn you, Jake," she said, to herself. "If I lose the trainee's job, it's all your fault."

At the very least, he could've phoned.

Jake got the *Alton Gazette* on his way home from the post office on Friday morning. Outside the newsagent's, he turned to the features section, felt a kick in his guts when he saw nothing about his recording session. Having talked to Tony, he knew how important publicity was, how much even a story in a local paper could help. If he got airplay on the local radio station, there was a chance that some of the big London DJs who lived in Surrey might hear the record and decide to play it themselves. The story about the recording session would have, could have helped.

He shook his head, thinking that Kerry wasn't vindictive, she wouldn't have dropped the story out of spite. Something must have gone wrong.

He thought for a long time before he decided to go and see her at the mall, before he went on to play his spot. He wanted to tell her how much she meant to him, to try to get the relationship on a firmer footing than it was now, with them seeing each other just by chance. He hoped for so much when they went to the recording session together, that they'd have time to work something out, but Kerry's friend had ruined it. Jake had hoped she wouldn't come, but she did. Worse, she virtually tricked him into agreeing to go to the Music Channel Party with her. Kerry didn't know that he had changed his mind afterwards, she'd already run away by then.

Jake was waiting outside the newspaper office when Kerry came out just after three o'clock.

"Hi," he said, shyly.

"Uh, hi," she said. She looked taken aback.

"I'm sorry about Wednesday. Not being at the mall. I had to go to London, y'see, to see a manager about my contract. I was supposed to see him at two, but I had to wait. I did ring you at the paper, but you'd already gone. I didn't actually get to see the guy until five, and I didn't get back here until nearly midnight."

"I see," Kerry said, in a neutral voice.

Jake squirmed inside. She wasn't making it easy for him. "You didn't do a story," he said, slowly.

Kerry winced. "I did, but … it wasn't right. I've done it again, though. With any luck, it'll be in the paper next week."

Jake struggled to smile, but all that came out was a little half-curve of his lips. "It all helps, you know. Publicity, I mean."

"I'll do the best I can," she said.

"D'you have time for a coffee?" Jake blurted.

She shook her head. "Sorry, but I'm meeting Zoey."

"Oh," Jake said.

Kerry smiled brightly. "See you around, then."

"Yeah," he said. "See you."

She turned to walk away.

Jake called her back. "Kerry?"

"Yes?"

"I didn't go to the Music Channel Party after all. I … I told Corinne that I couldn't make it just after you left. I tried to go after you but you'd already gone."

"Corinne told me what happened," Kerry said, coldly.

"Right," Jake said. "See you at the mall later."

"Maybe," Kerry said, then she turned and left.

Jake walked away slowly, letting the summer breeze cool the heat on his face. "I blew it," he said, to himself. "I really blew it."

He was quite sure that she didn't like him at all.

10

"What's the matter?" Zoey asked Kerry, when they'd been round all the driving schools.

She shrugged and shook her head, she didn't want to talk about it.

"Come on," Zoey said, "you've gone all quiet again."

"Jake lied to me," Kerry said.

Zoey gripped her arm and led her into the café on the High Street. It was quieter there than the mall.

"What happened?"

"You know how Corinne said she changed her mind about going to the Music Channel Party with him? Well, he said it was him who changed his mind about going with her."

"How d'you mean?"

"Well, as soon as we got to Alton, I just jumped out of the limo and ran. Corinne rang me later at the paper and said she'd decided not to go with him after all. Then this afternoon, he was outside the office when I left work. He said that he was the one who told Corinne that he didn't want to go, he said he told her in the limo after I left..."

Zoey drank her coffee. She was deep in thought. "I think it's Corinne who's lying," she said. "I wouldn't put it past her. If Jake did do that, change his mind, she'd be pretty mad about it. Who knows what she'd do? I don't think Corinne's ever been turned down in her life before. That morning in the mall, she had an odd look on her face. And she wanted to give you that dress, so she was feeling guilty about something."

"D'you think so?" Kerry asked.

Zoey lifted her eyebrows. "I do. If she and Jake are saying different things, between the two of them, I'd believe Jake."

"Oh *no!*" Kerry groaned. "I was icy cold with him. He wanted to go for a coffee, and I said no. What do I do now?"

Zoey took a deep breath. "I don't know..."

"Honestly, I could kill Corinne. I really could."

Zoey shook her head. "It's bad, even by her standards."

Kerry sighed. "I mean, she's got so many boys. What does she want with Jake? She didn't even like him until she found out he was getting a recording contract."

"Y'see," said Zoey, "she's got competition now. It was always the three of us, and Julie and I both had boyfriends. Then you came along, and Corinne realized that she wasn't the only attractive girl around."

"You and Julie are attractive too," Kerry said quickly.

"Maybe. But the fact is, Julie and I are taken, more or less. We're not interested in other boys. It was pretty clear to me from watching Jake watching you in the mall that he really likes you. I think Corinne noticed that, and she got jealous. Then you all go to London, and she finds out he's going to be a star. She wants what she can't have, she's so predictable, she's pathetic, in a way."

"Pathetic? I don't think so, not after what she's done to Jake and me."

"Kerry, she hasn't done anything, not really. Jake still likes you, or else he wouldn't've bothered to talk to you today."

"It's all such a mess, Zoey."

"No, it isn't."

Kerry finished her coffee. "So," she said, "what do I do now?"

"About Jake? I don't know," Zoey said. "Maybe you could ask him for a coffee or something yourself. Since he's asked you and you couldn't go."

"Maybe," Kerry said.

"Why not? You've got nothing to lose but your pride."

Kerry thought about it all Sunday night. She knew that Jake wasn't working then, that he'd be at home. Several times, she went to the phone, but although her finger hovered over the buttons, she never quite got around to dialling his number.

She was fairly certain now that he was shy, and she didn't want to push him. She kept on thinking, hoping, that he'd ask her again. If he did, she'd definitely go.

Kerry had never thought of herself as being shy. She was bright and bubbly, she thought, not quite certain of herself but reasonably sure. But, as time passed that week, she began to realize that she was shy as well; she found it incredibly difficult to bring herself to ring Jake up when all she had to say was to ask him if he'd like to come for a coffee with her.

She was very busy at work. The council had at last come up with a new traffic plan, and the editor sent her out around Alton with a copy of the plan to ask people what they thought of it. The *Alton Gazette* was very proud of its surveys, and she needed to interview one hundred local people by Wednesday afternoon, the deadline for the news section.

Kerry tried to throw herself into her work, not to think about Jake too much. The editor had finally read her rewritten story; he told her that it was really good and that he planned to run it as the front page lead of the feature section, with a big colour picture of Jake.

Kerry was deeply relieved; her career plans were on track again and Jake would be pleased with the publicity. She decided to wait until Friday before she talked to him, because then she had a really good excuse; Zoey's birthday was on Sunday and she was having a barbecue in the garden, it would be just perfect if Jake could go with her.

Kerry spent all week planning what she would say: she didn't go to the mall in the afternoons, saying that she was busy although the real reason was that she didn't want to see Corinne. She and Zoey usually had lunch together instead.

She even missed Jake's spot on Wednesday, because she was so busy with the story about the traffic plan. Zoey agreed to explain that to Jake, and afterwards she phoned Kerry to say that he looked disappointed when she gave him the news.

On Thursday, after the paper had gone to the printer's, the editor always took the staff for a meal to celebrate. That week, for the first time, he asked Kerry to come too. Both he and the news editor told her that she had done well with the survey, and she was very pleased with herself.

They went to a Chinese restaurant, where the editor ordered dozens of different dishes which they all shared. Kerry sat, drinking in the atmosphere and enjoying the stories.

The evening ended too quickly, at ten o'clock when some of the die-hards went on to the pub and Kerry left to go home.

On Friday, she was the first in the office, apart from the receptionist. She opened the paper eagerly, then felt her heart sink when she saw the front page of the features section. The lead story was all about a young athlete from Alton, who had just broken the European sprint record for boys of his age. The copy trumpeted that he was a future gold medallist, and that he was training hard for the next Olympic Games.

Jake had been consigned to a photo on the lower half of the page, her copy cut to a few paragraphs which ran alongside it.

Kerry felt sick, hoped that he would not see it as a snub.

Jake paced his basement studio, from wall to wall. He was doing a lot of pacing these days. If his thoughts weren't on Kerry, then they were on his recording contract: most of all, what would happen when his single was released.

Brutal statistics said that it would sink like a stone, sell only a couple of hundred copies through the local shops in Alton. That was what happened to most records by new artistes; if it happened to Jake, he'd no doubts that Reflex wouldn't take up the option in his contract to do an album.

Jake had his contract now. It had arrived that morning, along with a long letter from Tony Steiger explaining the details and outlining his options. Although Jake had read it many times, he read it again now, unable to believe what he was seeing.

The contract gave him a payment of £2,500; once Tony's percentage was deducted, that gave him £2,000, more money than he'd ever had before in his life. The money was actually an advance against the royalties that he would get once the record went on sale; for every record that was sold, Jake would get 20p. It was the implications of that tiny amount that worried him; to make the deal worthwhile for Reflex, Jake's record had to sell at least 10,000 copies.

Ten thousand copies, Jake thought. Will it make it? Will *I* make it?

To sell that many, the record needed airplay far

beyond the tiny local station in Alton. It needed to make it on the big regional stations, and the nationals like Virgin and Atlantic 252, most of all, Radio 1.

Tony said that Radio 1 no longer mattered so much, with all the other stations that networked chart shows, but it had been on Radio 1 that Jake had first listened to pop music, and then learned about it; it had always been his ambition to hear his own record there.

The contract was still unsigned. He read it a final time, then initialled all the pages and signed the last one; he got his sister to witness it. He'd thought of asking Kerry, but maybe that was presuming too much.

There was still one final thing to do. The record didn't have a title yet, *The Girl With The Smile In Her Eyes* was only the working title – Tim Sloan thought it was a bit long to be the title when the record was released. Most records, he said, have only one or two words in the title, a maximum of three.

Jake had thought about it for a long time, and discussed his idea with Tony and Tim Sloan, both of whom liked it.

With trembling fingers, Jake filled in the blank space that had been left on the contract.

Kerry's Song, he wrote.

Afterwards, he sat still for a long time, thinking about her. Although her coldness last week had hurt him, he thought that it was only fair to name the song after her, because she had been its inspiration.

There was a nice ring about it: *Kerry's Song*.

Jake put the contract in the envelope then took it to the post office, where he mailed it first class. Then he dropped in at the *trattoria*, where Mario was busy preparing the *osso bucco* for the evening menu.

"Ow ees our pop star?" Mario asked him.

Jake cleared his throat nervously, then told him that his manager wanted him to play some gigs in the London clubs, to try to drum up interest in his new single. Although he didn't want to give up his dishwashing job just yet, he wondered if Mario could let him have a few nights off.

"Sure, no problem," Mario said. "I am glad to 'elp our young pop star."

Jake grinned broadly. He deeply appreciated his boss's support.

"You let me know, first engagement," Mario said. "Gina and me, we like to come and see you."

"Sunday, in the Bistro 92 in Wardour Street," he said. Tony had arranged the gig for him – it wasn't a big venue, he said, but live music was a feature on Sunday nights and a lot of people in the record business went there.

"I be there weeth Gina," Mario said.

"Great," said Jake, "see you then."

He went home whistling *Kerry's Song*, thinking that he'd see the real Kerry that afternoon at the mall. Jake was looking forward to it. He had decided to ask her to the Bistro to see his gig; although it didn't finish until late, he knew that Mario would give them both a lift home.

* * *

Kerry's mouth was dry, her hands were shaky. She'd agreed to meet Zoey at the mall just after work, long before Corinne turned up. She was going to ask Jake to Zoey's party: she'd planned what she was going to say so carefully that she was afraid that it would sound like a speech.

Before they went to the café, they went to the party shop where Zoey bought lots of aerosol streamers and funny paper hats. Zoey hesitated over the custom-printed T-shirts, as Kerry tried to pry her away from them without seeming too obvious, because her own present to her friend was a jumbo T-shirt printed with Zoey, The World's Greatest Seventeen-Year-Old on one side, and Zoey, The World's Best Friend on the other. Kerry had chosen the design of fake newspaper headlines over a picture of Zoey, and she hoped the slogans would make her smile.

"I'd really like one," Zoey said, as Kerry eventually managed to interest her in a display of joke glasses that you couldn't really drink out of. "But they're kind of expensive. I'll just have to hope that someone gives me one."

Kerry smiled to herself.

Once they'd bought their cappuccinos, they sat down on the stools outside the coffee bar, because all the tables were taken.

"Hmm," said Zoey. "It's very busy. It's probably your story about Jake."

Kerry winced at the mention of it. She felt really bad about how it had been cut, although her reporter's instinct told her that the young athlete was a better story. She was still ashamed over the missed deadline, although the editor's praise later had made her feel a bit better about herself.

"I'm thinking of finishing with Simon," Zoey said.

Kerry looked at her. She'd sensed for a while that things were going wrong, or, at least, not as right as they'd once been. When she'd known Zoey at first, she'd talked about Simon a lot; now, she rarely mentioned him.

"How come?" Kerry said. It was a big step for Zoey, especially after she'd been going out with him for so long.

"Well, part of it is seeing you with Jake. You're really crazy about him, and I don't feel that way about Simon any more. We've been together for ages, it's just sort of fading out. At least, it is for me. His parents are going on holiday and he's staying at home, and he keeps on dropping these heavy hints that I should stay with him, you know?"

Kerry nodded.

Zoey sighed. "I thought about it, and I realized that I just don't feel that way about him. A couple of times, when Chris's brought his friends home, I see one, and I think, he's nice. I wouldn't be thinking that at all if I was happy with Simon."

"I see," Kerry said, twisting a strand of her hair into a dreadlock and then unravelling it again.

Suddenly, she gulped. "I've just had a horrible thought," she said.

"What?"

"If Jake and I, if we do get together, and then if you split up with Simon, you'll be all on your own Saturday nights."

"Not exactly," Zoey said, grinning. "There's always Corinne."

Kerry laughed.

"I was thinking, after my party, I'll suggest that we cool it a bit."

"If you're sure, I mean, if you've thought it through."

"That's just it, Kerry. It's not thinking so much as feeling. My feelings have changed, and there's not much I can do."

"I've just had another horrible thought," Kerry said.

Zoey looked at her. "What is it this time?"

"If Simon's going to be nasty about it, he'll just say that you didn't split with him before your birthday because you wanted your present from him."

"Gee," said Zoey. "I can't wait. At Christmas I get bubble bath. Birthdays I get talcum powder. Nothing fancy, just Yardley. I mean, how can I live without it?"

They laughed.

"Just give it back to him," Kerry said. "He can give it to his next girlfriend."

Zoey glanced at the clock. "It's nearly a quarter to," she said. "You'd better get moving."

They'd planned it that Kerry would leave the mall at the coffee shop exit and walk along the road, so she'd meet Jake well away from any possible interruptions, such as Corinne. She also wanted to be alone, she was so nervous that she didn't want anyone to see her.

Kerry walked along the road for a bit and then turned back towards the mall. She wasn't sure what direction Jake was coming from, so she couldn't go too far. When she got back to the mall entrance, she checked her watch: it was fourteen minutes to five. Sighing, she began to walk along the road again and then she saw him at the pedestrian crossing, his guitar case in hand.

He saw her at once, and waved cheerfully, gesturing as if he wanted her to wait for him.

Kerry's heart skipped a beat.

When the lights changed, he ran across the road.

"Hi," he said.

"Hi," she replied, telling herself not to get her hopes up; he hadn't rung her at work, after all.

They both started to speak at once.

"I'm sorry..." said Kerry.

"Thanks for the story," Jake said.

They laughed and gazed at each other.

"The story," Kerry said. "It was cut. It should've been much longer, but that story about the athlete came in."

"I thought it was great," Jake said.

"We'll do another one when your record comes out."

"That'll be September."

"So long?"

"It's soon, actually," Jake said. "They're designing the cover now. I've to go up to London next week to be photographed. Then it's all got to be proofed and printed. But September's quite a good time for it. The week they're releasing it, there're no mega-sellers coming out. You know, nothing by the big guys. So I'm hoping some of the DJs will listen to it."

Kerry grinned. It was coming to the time to ask him, and the butterflies in her stomach felt like a flock of geese.

"I was wondering…" she said, her voice tailing off, as her courage faltered.

Jake looked at her, smiling. She thought she detected interest in his eyes.

"Yes?" he said.

"Zoey's seventeen on Sunday and she's having a barbecue. Would you like to come? It'll just be casual, no dressing up. You don't even have to bring your guitar!"

Jake's face had fallen and Kerry felt her heart sink.

"I'm really sorry," he said, "but my manager – I've got a manager now – he's fixed me up with a gig in London. I've already said I'd do it, so I can't cancel. I was going to ask you if you'd like to come with me."

"Oh, no," Kerry said. "I would, Jake, really I would, but Zoey's my best friend and … and I need to be there, I really do." His expression was unreadable and she wondered for a moment if he'd asked her just to be nice, and not because he wanted her to come.

He smiled. "Some other time, then, sometime soon?"

"Yes. Of course," Kerry said.

They began to walk towards the mall. In the distance, Kerry saw Corinne coming from the other direction. She waved brightly, then headed into the mall. Kerry realized that Jake was no longer walking by her side; she turned and saw that he had dipped behind a display of vegetables outside the greengrocer's. When he emerged, he grinned guiltily.

Kerry's courage surged. I have to know, she thought. "Jake," she said, carefully, "Corinne said that *she* was the one who changed her mind about the gig."

"What?" Surprise was written all over his face, he couldn't have faked it.

"Yes," said Kerry. "She said she told you just after I got out of the car."

Jake frowned. "I told *her*, Kerry. The way she asked me, it was almost impossible to refuse. Then you took off. I told her that I'd just remembered I had something else to do that day. She was really mad. She slammed the door of the limo so hard that the whole thing shook."

"Oh," Kerry said, thinking, was there anything that Corinne wouldn't do?

"I felt really bad about it afterwards," Jake said. He was about to tell her about the hundreds of phone calls he'd made, but his shyness stopped him.

They reached the entrance to the mall.

"See you soon," Jake said.

"Yes, see you," Kerry said, struggling to keep the disappointment out of her voice.

"I'll ring you," Jake said.

Kerry managed a tiny smile. They reached the coffee bar, where they had to part.

"I don't have your number," Jake said. He hated to lie, but he'd tell her the truth later, when they got to know each other better.

"650259," Kerry said.

He fumbled in his pocket and found a pen to write it down.

"I'll ring you," he said again.

Kerry was thrilled.

11

"Oh, Kerry," Zoey said, when she'd opened her present and found the T-shirt inside, "it's wonderful. I'm going to wear it soon's I've finished with the barbecue."

Kerry smiled. Zoey had asked her to come early, to help her get ready for her party. The barbecue was already lit, the charcoal glowing, and they'd set out plenty of paper plates and cups. The salads were chilling in the fridge, and the potatoes baking slowly in the oven. Zoey was expecting about thirty guests, maybe a few more. Her parents were staying in the house, although they had promised to keep well out of the way.

Zoey and Kerry were both wearing T-shirts and jeans; they didn't want to have to worry about their clothes when they were cooking on a spitting barbecue.

Zoey took a final look around the garden. It was a beautiful day, the sun shining in a flawless sky with just a hint of a breeze so that it wasn't too hot.

"I think we're ready," she said.

"It's perfect," Kerry told her.

They moved to the drive, to greet Zoey's guests. Her parents wanted to say hello to everyone, then they'd leave them alone. They hadn't given Zoey her present yet, her father insisted on saying a few words when everybody had arrived. Zoey was deeply embarrassed, but she didn't argue with him.

It was five to five, and the invitations said the party would start at five.

"This is the bit I hate," Zoey said. "You're standing here wondering if anyone's going to come."

Kerry laughed. "They'll come," she said, "they'd be crazy not to."

Julie and Mike came first. They handed Zoey a gift-wrapped package as Kerry poured them a drink.

"This is from both of us," Julie said.

"Wow," Zoey said, when she'd unwrapped the parcel. It was a pair of leather driving gloves. "They're beautiful, but you shouldn't've."

"I'm glad you like them," Mike grinned. Once they had their drinks, they moved into the garden, where they stood gazing at each other as if the world beyond them didn't exist.

A crowd of their school friends came next. They'd pooled their money to buy Zoey a pair of Levis. She was thrilled.

Kerry nudged her. Simon had just driven up in his father's car, which he parked in the street outside. He was a year older than Zoey, he'd passed his test a few months before.

He kissed Zoey on the lips, then handed her a big parcel. Kerry saw a frown flutter across her friend's face.

"Aren't you going to open it?" Simon asked her.

"Of course," she said.

It was a sweater, knitted in a dozen different colours. Kerry gasped. She'd seen it in the mall, she knew what it cost.

Zoey said nothing.

"Don't you like it?" Simon asked her.

"I … yes, I love it, but, Simon, you should't've."

"Only the best's good enough for my girl," he said, putting a proprietorial arm around her shoulder. Zoey looked uncomfortable, but there was nothing she could do.

Corinne came, with a big bottle of CK One, then more friends with CDs and book tokens, and some of Chris's friends, who'd brought Zoey a season ticket for the health club.

"I think that's everybody," she said, once she'd thanked them and all the guests were all gathered in the garden. Simon still had his arm around her shoulders.

Kerry stopped her from leaving the drive. She couldn't believe her eyes. Jake was walking up the drive towards them, holding an envelope and a bunch of flowers.

He said hi first to Kerry, then he handed the card and the flowers to Zoey. "I just wanted to say, Happy Birthday," he said, "and I'm sorry I couldn't come to your party."

"That doesn't matter," Zoey said. She was thrilled with the flowers; it was the first time anyone had given her a bouquet. "D'you have time for a drink?"

"Sorry," Jake said. "I've got to get the five-twenty train. The gig doesn't start until seven, but I need to be there at half-six."

Kerry and Zoey wished him good luck. Simon's eyes followed him jealously as he walked back down the drive.

In the garden, Zoey's father tapped a glass. The hum of conversation ceased.

"I know I'm not invited," he said, "but Helly, Zoey's mother, and I, we just wanted to tell you all to have a good time. And, of course, to wish Zoey a Happy Birthday."

"Happy Birthday!" everyone said.

Zoey blushed.

"Your present's in the garage, Zoey, if you want to go and have a look at it," he said. Looking puzzled, Zoey went round to the side of the house, where Simon helped her open the overhead garage door. Inside was a shiny Volkswagen Polo, a few years old but in such good condition it looked brand new.

Zoey was too stunned to speak, then she threw her arms around her father and hugged him, and then she hugged her mother too.

"D'you like it?" her father asked her.

"I love it," she said, tears streaming down her cheeks. "But it's too much."

Her father grinned. "It worked out cheaper in the end, rather than pay the insurance for you to drive mine."

Zoey's parents left then and the party got under

way in earnest. Kerry brought out the salads and bowls of crisps, while Simon helped Zoey with the barbecue.

Simon stayed at Zoey's side, as if he was glued to her. A couple of times, she and Kerry managed to exchange looks; Zoey raised her eyes to the sky, as if to ask, what can I do? Finally, she managed to get rid of him for a few minutes by asking him to get the baked potatoes.

"I feel terrible about the sweater," she said.

"You can give it back to him. He'll get his money back."

"He's being so nice. I feel so terrible when I know I'm going to tell him that it's all off tomorrow."

"I know," Kerry said. "At least, I don't know, but I can imagine."

Once everybody had been served, Kerry helped herself to some jerk chicken and salad. She sat down with some of the girls from school, who were talking to a group of Chris's friends. Because her anger was simmering over what she'd said about Jake, Kerry wanted to avoid Corinne. If she had a row with her, it would spoil the party, and she'd feel hypocritical if she pretended that she didn't know what Corinne had done.

As soon as Kerry sat down, though, Corinne left the boy she was talking to and came and sat down besides her.

"Good party," Corinne said.

"Yes," Kerry agreed.

As Corinne talked, Kerry concentrated on her food. When she finished, the boy who was sitting next to her asked her if he could get her some more.

"Thanks," Kerry said, grateful that when he came back she'd have an excuse to talk to him.

"You're very quiet," Corinne said.

"Am I?"

"As if you're upset about something. Is anything wrong?"

Kerry fumbled for something to say. Frantically, she looked around, saw the boy standing in line with her plate.

"I'd better go and help him," she said, getting up.

Corinne began to say something else, but Kerry didn't wait to hear what it was.

On Monday afternoon, Kerry waited anxiously for Zoey in the open air café just outside the mall. There was a heatwave, and it was too hot to be inside.

Corinne arrived before Zoey.

"I was waiting in the mall," she said, petulantly. "You didn't tell me you were going to be here. I had to guess!"

Kerry sighed. She hadn't told Corinne deliberately and neither had Zoey. They wanted to talk about Simon alone.

Corinne sat down, ordering a lemon *frappé*.

"I spoke to Jake," Kerry said.

"Oh?" Corinne said.

"He said that *he* was the one who decided not to go to the party."

Corinne shrugged. "I can't remember really. As

soon as I saw how upset you were, I changed my mind about it. I can't remember exactly who said what. It doesn't matter anyhow."

"I'd rather you hadn't lied," Kerry said, carefully.

"It's nothing, Kerry. He's just a boy. In any case, guess what?"

"I'm not really interested," Kerry said, coldly.

Corinne froze a moment. "Look, Kerry, I upset you, I know, I was wrong, but I said sorry. You don't have to be like that. I mean, we're still friends."

"Are we?"

"Well, of course we are."

Kerry shook her head. "I trust my friends, and I don't trust you."

Corinne sat for a moment, her lips twisted into an anxious twitch, then she stood up and strode away.

Zoey came at last. She looked pale. As she sat down, Kerry asked the waitress to bring her an iced coffee. When it came, she drank it slowly.

"I talked to Simon," she said, finally.

"I guessed. Was it tough?"

Zoey nodded. "It was just like you said. He accused me of not telling him sooner just because I didn't want to spoil my party. I gave him the sweater back, but he just threw it at me, told me to keep it. I feel really lousy about hurting him."

"You'd feel worse if you stayed with him when you didn't want to."

"I know. I just wish it didn't have to be this way."

Kerry smiled.

"I mean, what do I do with the sweater?"

"I suppose you could take it back and give him the money, or send it to him."

"I suppose."

They went back to the shop and returned the sweater, and eventually got a refund after filling in a form and giving Zoey's name and address. Zoey put the money into an envelope and they took it round to Simon's and left it for him.

"Oh, well, that's it," Zoey said. "The end of a beautiful friendship."

"Or the beginning of a new one."

They linked arms and began to walk along the road.

"Oh, by the way, I met Corinne coming out the mall," Zoey said. "She said, 'I don't know what's got into Kerry, she's turned into a real bitch!'"

Kerry laughed. "Come on," she said, "there's a new movie on. It's a comedy, it's meant to be really good."

"Has Jake called yet?"

"Not yet. There's a showing at 4.45, if we go, it'll take my mind off thinking about it."

When she got in later, there was a message scrawled on the board besides the kitchen phone.

Jake called at half past six. Said he'd call back.

The thrill made Kerry jump up and down. Then she calmed down a little, wondered when he'd call back. Although the message was in her mother's writing, the house was empty, she must have gone shopping or something.

Kerry settled down to wait, watching the seconds tick by on the big kitchen clock.

Seven-fifteen came, then seven-thirty. Come on, she thought, if he didn't call soon, the house would be full of people and she didn't want anyone to listen in to their conversation. Kerry wondered whether to call him then decided to wait a little longer.

At twenty to eight she heard the sound of her mother's car coming into the driveway. The phone rang just then. For a moment, Kerry was so surprised that she didn't react, then she rushed through to her father's study to use the extension there.

For a split second, the phone became a snake, that would bite her if she touched it.

Kerry steeled herself, then picked up the receiver.

"H-hello?" she said.

"Kerry?" It was Jake's voice.

Kerry held her hand over the mouthpiece and sighed with relief.

"I rang earlier, but you weren't in yet. The paper said you'd already left."

"I was with Zoey," she said.

"Of course," he said.

Kerry heard the door closing, and then her mother beginning to put away shopping in the kitchen.

"Thing is," Jake said, "I was wondering if you'd like to come for a coffee sometime? I don't have much time in the evenings, but I'm free in the afternoons. We could meet up after work, if you like. If you don't have to see Zoey."

"I don't see Zoey every day," Kerry said quickly, knowing that Zoey would forgive her.

"Well, you pick a day, then," Jake said. "If you'd like to, that is?"

Kerry thought frantically. Wednesdays were always busy at the paper, and so were Thursdays if there was a late-breaking story. That left only tomorrow or Friday. Tomorrow was too soon, she thought, and Friday was almost a week away.

"I'd like to," she said, "but sometimes I have to stay late at the paper on Wednesdays and Thursdays..." Her voice tailed off, she was afraid that it might sound like she was discouraging him.

"What about tomorrow?" he said.

Kerry's heart fluttered. "That'd be great, Jake."

"I'll meet you outside the *Gazette* office at three?"

"Yes," she said. "I'll see you then."

12

Jake was waiting when Kerry left work the next day. He grinned when he saw her, and she was struck by how gorgeous he was. His hair still flopped in that unruly way across his brow, and there was a faint hint of stubble on his chin, as if he had forgotten to shave. He was wearing jeans and trainers, and a white shirt which shone brightly against his slightly tanned skin. His sweater was thrown casually over his shoulder.

"Hi," he said, "I was thinking, it's a lovely day, and there's this wonderful place just along the river. We could hire a boat and row there, if you've got time."

"I've got the rest of the day," Kerry said.

As they walked down to the river, Kerry drank in the pleasure of being alone with him for a couple of hours. Neither of them said anything until they reached the jetty where the boats were tied up, but each time their eyes met they smiled at each other.

Jake paid for the boat, then helped her in. Kerry felt guilty because it cost £5; she decided she'd pay for their coffees, or whatever they'd have. Although the contract was signed, she was pretty sure that Jake hadn't got the money yet.

Skilfully, he manoeuvred the boat away from the jetty and into the middle of the river. He rowed well, and she watched the muscles in his forearms move as he worked the oars.

"How did your gig go?" she asked him, after a moment. She'd meant to ask him when he phoned, but when she heard his voice the question just went out of her head.

"Good," he said. "The place is sort of a restaurant and bar. You know, some people were eating, some were just drinking. When I started to play the first number, they hardly noticed me. But then they stopped talking. Once I'd played a couple of numbers, they started to listen to me. It was really good. I was booked to play for an hour, but in the end I played for two. And they asked me back in a fortnight's time."

"It must be really frightening," she said, "to have to play to an audience."

"It is, in a way, but I really like doing it. You write a song, but you don't know whether it's any good or not until you play it to people. It's like, I don't know, the best way I can describe it is that you're sharing something with your audience. If it's a good song, you can see it on their faces, the way they listen. It's a nice feeling. At least, I like it."

"I wouldn't dare," Kerry said.

Jake shrugged. "I thought I didn't dare, too," he said, "then I realized that I'd been playing to my family and my music teachers for ages, so I might as well try. I did my first gig when I was at school; you know, the school concert. I was petrified. I was shaking all over, and my hands were so sweaty I could hardly hold the guitar. But then I did it and afterwards everybody clapped. I mean, the audience was all parents and teachers. They'd have clapped for Conan the Barbarian. But it broke the ice and it was easier the next time. It doesn't worry me now, except when it's important, like when I made the demo or when I did the gig on Sunday. I feel a bit nervous, but once I start to play, I feel fine."

Kerry smiled. "Why was the gig important?"

"It's this place in Wardour Street in Soho. Lots of people in the music business go there. There was a couple of DJs from Capital Radio there on Sunday. I'd've probably clammed up, 'cept I didn't know who they were until it was all over."

"You wouldn't clam up," she said, "you're too professional."

"I don't know," he said. "The funny thing is that I'm really shy, apart from playing music. I find it easier to play music to people than actually to talk to them. I mean, take you."

Kerry shivered inside.

"I noticed you at the mall ages ago," Jake said. "I really wanted to talk to you, but I didn't know what to say. So I used to sing to you instead."

Kerry felt the skin of her face redden as she remembered her dream. She was sitting facing

Jake, and the breeze was blowing the other way. She let her hand fall over the side of the boat and trail along the river, her fingers sending up droplets of water that glittered like diamonds in the light of the sun. Some of the droplets hit her face, cooling the blaze in her cheeks.

"Then Corinne dragged you up that day," Jake said.

"I know. I was really embarrassed."

He smiled. "At least, she got us talking to each other. God knows when that would've happened if it hadn't been for her."

Kerry suddenly felt a rush of gratitude; maybe, she thought, she'd forgive Corinne.

There were willow trees on either side of the water, their branches trailing into the river. It was a perfect day to be in a boat.

"So," Jake said, "where did you live before you came to Alton?"

She began to tell him about her life in Cumbria, about all the friends she'd left behind, about how sometimes she missed the wide open spaces, although she didn't miss the bitter winters or the rain that sometimes threatened to wash the road away.

The river turned, and then there was a little pub in a building that Kerry recognized was medieval. The walls were very thick and the windows were tiny, and the roof wasn't tiled, but thatched with straw.

"This is it," Jake said, as he manoeuvred the boat towards a jetty, where he tied it up and then helped her out.

They took a table outside, by the river.

"What would you like?" Jake asked Kerry.

"Please," she said, "let me."

He shook his head vigorously. "That's not fair. I asked you. I've got a recording contract, remember? Besides, it's our first date, if you count a row along the river as a date."

Kerry felt dizzy for a moment, then she asked for an orange juice, because it was too hot for coffee. She went into the pub with him, because she wanted to see what it was like inside.

The interior was a series of small rooms, some with tables laid for food, some just with soft chairs for people who didn't want to eat. The air smelled of lavender and wood smoke; although it was a very hot day, there were fires laid in every grate.

The bar was empty. Jake had to ring a bell before someone came to take his order.

"I like this place," he said. "I like the atmosphere."

"So do I," Kerry said.

The orange juices came, in tall glasses with ice and mint.

Kerry gasped when the bartender asked Jake for £6. She asked him again if he'd let her pay, or at least share the cost. He told her that he'd get really angry if she mentioned money again.

"Like I said, it's our first date," he said, once they'd settled down at the table outside. "I wanted it to be really special."

"It is," said Kerry. "It's very special."

She took a sip of her orange juice. It was freshly squeezed and perfectly chilled.

"Tell me about your manager," she said.

Jake took a deep breath, and then he began to tell her about Tony Steiger. Once he'd described his manager, he went on to talk about how difficult it was to make it in music even though he'd got a single coming out; about how, in the end, his future rested not with the single or the record company, but in the hands of a few powerful DJs.

"It's frightening," Kerry said, wondering how she could possibly help him.

"I know," he said. "And even if you make it with the first record, you can always bomb later."

Kerry hadn't realized that.

"If you even think of the charts last year," Jake said, "a lot of people fade overnight. They have a couple of hits, and then they're out of it. It's kind of hard, you know? I want to make music for the rest of my life, but I don't know if I'll be able to."

"I'm sure you will," she said, carefully.

Jake shrugged. "Tony said I could probably make it writing songs. Playing them, well, he wants me to work on some new material. He told me to try a couple of dance songs. He said that'll be good if he gets me a contract for an album. But first, the single has to sell."

Kerry shivered. Suddenly, she realized that the sun had fallen behind the inn; they were in shadow. A glance at her watch told her that it was nearly seven o'clock – she wondered where all the time had gone. They had been talking constantly for nearly three hours. She had sipped her drink very slowly, because she didn't want Jake to buy another one at £3 a go, but the ice had melted now, there was only water left in the glass.

Jake, too, had noticed the time.

"We'd better get going," he said. "I've got dishes to wash."

They got up and walked back to the boat. He helped her sit down, then he sat down himself and picked up the oars.

"Jake," she said, "listen to me. You're going to make it. You're too good not to. I mean, how many people your age have a manager? How many of them have a recording contract, even if it's only for a single?"

"That's just it. There's so much riding on the single."

"I know, but there's no law that says it has to be a mega-success. It's a good record, everyone knows that, so you've done your bit. I don't know much about music, but it seems to me that whether the record sells or not is mostly luck and how the record company promotes it and things like that, and you don't control these things. You can't. All you can do is go on making music. If you keep on doing that, sooner or later you'll get there. Just keep on trying, Jake. I know this record means an awful lot to you, but just be proud of it for what it is: your first record. Try not to worry about whether it gets airplay or not, or whether it sells or not, because all that's down to other people, not you."

He looked at her for a long time, until she was worried that she'd said the wrong thing, and wondering what she could say to make it right.

"Jake, I…" she began.

He held a finger to her lips to silence her. "You

just spoke sense, Kerry. A helluva lot of sense. Thanks."

They didn't talk on the way back. Kerry sat in the boat, enjoying the sensation of floating down the river, most of all, of being with Jake.

He walked her all the way home. In a way, he was old-fashioned, he had the kind of good manners that Kerry's grandmother would appreciate; he held doors open for her, held her chair for her as she sat down, things like that.

Kerry loved being with him.

"Thanks, Jake, I had a really great time," she said, as they stood outside the gate of her house. There wasn't time to ask him in for a coffee.

"Good," he said, smiling. "So did I."

She turned to leave him, deeply disappointed that he hadn't asked her out again.

"Kerry," he said, calling her back.

She waited.

"Uh, I'd really like to see you again soon, but I'm really busy working on new material for gigs. Tony's talking about one in Manchester at the weekend, and I've to go to Reflex for a photo-session for the cover. So I'll call you, right?"

Kerry smiled. "That'll be nice."

"And thanks again for what you said. It made me feel a lot better. It really did."

Jake left her, thinking that he'd like it if she could be with him as he worked on his new songs. The thing was, although he loved the process of writing music, he knew that it was boring for someone listening, because he kept stopping and starting, repeating phrases until he got it right.

His old girlfriend had told him that.

Maybe, he thought, he could ask her later, once he had got to know her better. He'd been right all along about Kerry. She *was* different. He liked her a lot, more than a lot, and now he knew that he needed her as well.

She was so important to him that he didn't want to mess it up.

Jake thought that he hadn't a lot to offer a girl, only a dream of distant moonshine really: the infinitesimally small chance that one of his songs would make it and he'd become like normal people with a little money to spend and time as well, because he'd be free of the constant pressure to succeed.

All he knew was that if he didn't make it at first, he'd go on trying, busking around and sending off demo tapes, washing dishes and delivering mail in between times, doing whatever he had to do to keep his dream alive. His dream wasn't of mega-stardom, just of making a living with his songs.

So he didn't have much to promise a girl like Kerry. But then, she'd just about said it herself – his first record didn't have to be a mega-seller, it just had to be the best that he could do, and it *was* that.

She wouldn't have said that if she hadn't been prepared to go along with him, whatever happened.

He began to whistle a tune as he went into the *trattoria* and headed for the pile of dishes in the kitchen.

Kerry understood, she really did. Jake knew that she was right for him, he just had to make sure that he got it right with her.

Kerry drifted through the week in a dream. Now she knew that he liked her, or, she was pretty sure that he did, she thought she just had to wait, give him space. There was so much on his mind with the record, she wanted to help so much, but she sensed that he needed time to work it all out.

She wanted to wave a magic wand and send his record straight to No. 1, but she couldn't do that.

And waiting wasn't always easy, when she ached to be with him.

She told Zoey all about her afternoon with him. Corinne was away in New York with her father; she'd sent a postcard but Kerry didn't really care about her any more. For a while, she had been really mad with Corinne, but her anger faded because her mind was full of thoughts of Jake.

Corinne didn't matter any more.

Jake called on Thursday night. "That gig in Manchester," he said, "I'm doing it on Sunday night. It's a club, there's lots of different acts. Tony says a lot of the big DJs go to it."

Kerry gripped the phone tightly. She was getting used to the tyranny of the DJs.

"It'd be really nice if you could come," Jake said, "but it doesn't finish till really late and I'll have to stay over and get the first train back in the morning."

She was thinking, desperately wondering if she could find a way. Her parents wouldn't be happy about her being away overnight, especially if she was going with a boy they didn't know.

"Maybe you can come next time," Jake said.

"I'd really like that," she said, lamely, thinking that if he actually asked her to come to Manchester, she'd find a way of getting there.

Jake talked a bit about the new songs he was writing, then he said he'd have to go because he had to get to the *trattoria*.

"See you tomorrow at the mall," he said.

"Yes," Kerry said, "see you tomorrow."

"Hang on," he said, as she was about to hang up, "I won't be on until six. I've swapped spots with Keith, you know? He's helped me out a few times, and he needs an earlier spot tomorrow night."

"OK," Kerry said, her heart sinking because she'd hoped she could spend some time with him before he had to go to his dishwashing job.

On Friday, she sat with Zoey, listening to Jake as he sang some of his new songs. Kerry liked them all, loved one so much that she hummed the tune along with him, even though she had a terrible singing voice.

As usual at the mall, some people asked him to play their favourites; that frustrated her because she'd rather listen to the music he wrote himself.

The spot didn't end until after seven. Zoey left discreetly and Kerry made sure she had an ice-cold Coke waiting for Jake.

He was so hot that a sheen of sweat damped the locks of hair that flopped over his forehead. He drained the Coke in one.

"I did the photo-session this afternoon," he said. "How did it go?"

Jake sighed. "You wouldn't believe it. They wanted me to have designer stubble, so they told me not to shave for a few days. When I got there, they took some shots – they do polaroids at the same time so they know what the finished shot is going to look like – then they decided they wanted me clean-shaven, so they got this hairdresser to cut it all off. I mean, a hairdresser? As if I couldn't't've shaved it off myself? Then, when they saw the polaroids of that, they decided I looked better with the stubble, so I've got to let it grow again and do the same thing next week."

Kerry laughed.

"I mean, I only play songs. I never pretended to be a model."

Kerry thought that, either way, he looked good enough to eat.

"What did you think of the new material?"

"I really liked it. The tunes are really good."

"The lyrics suck. I know."

"Jake! I didn't say that, and I didn't mean it."

He sighed. "The song – that's the tune – always comes first. It takes time to work out the words."

Kerry gazed at him. She was thrilled just to be with him. He asked her all about her work, how things were going at the newspaper. She told him about that, and a little about Zoey, who was trying to get used to life without a steady boyfriend.

"Hey," he said, "once I get this single out of the way, you must bring her along to the college dances. There're never enough girls."

Kerry's heart skipped at the knowledge that he was thinking of her so far ahead.

Too soon, the time came when they had to part.

"I'll be in Manchester on Sunday," he said, "but I'll call you next week."

"OK," she said.

13

Next week, after the paper had finally gone to bed, the editor asked Kerry into his office for a chat.

"You're leaving us soon," he said, "I just wanted to thank you for all your good work. I'll put in a word for you when you go for the trainee job."

Kerry thanked him dully. She'd completely forgotten that her parents had planned the family holiday for the last two weeks of August. She couldn't bear to think of being away that long and not seeing Jake. Numbly, she wondered if she could wriggle out of it, stay at home instead. They usually went to Cornwall, or camping in France; the very idea of it was as thrilling as a rain-cloud.

"These pieces you did on that busker were really good," the editor said. "I was wondering if you'd like to do a column every month? Something like, The Young Scene by Kerry Smith."

What a terrible title, Kerry thought, wincing at Jake being called a busker. "I'd like to do that," she said.

"Just four or five hundred words. We'll pay you the union rate. It's not much but it's more than pocket money."

Kerry thanked him.

"I really think you've got a future in this business," he said.

She left the office and went to the mall, where Zoey was waiting.

As she sipped her coffee, Kerry thought, this is all wrong, the way I'm feeling. I'm going on seventeen, and I've been offered a newspaper column.

She told Zoey all about it, then asked her to go for a pizza to celebrate.

"You look pretty glum for a girl on the threshold of a glittering career," Zoey said, as they waited for the *calzoni*.

Kerry sighed, and cupped her chin in her hands. "We're going on holiday next week, I mean, the Smith family holiday to wonderful Penzance or Normandy or wherever. Like Boresville, wherever it is."

"I see," Zoey said.

"Do you? It means a whole *two weeks* without seeing Jake."

"Ah."

The *calzoni* came. Kerry stabbed hers with a fork as if it was the holiday that she didn't want.

"You could stay with me," Zoey said, "except we're going to Wales, so you'd be away from Jake the same way."

Kerry groaned.

There was a very happy atmosphere in her house

that night and Kerry noticed it as soon as she opened the front door.

Her little brother was engrossed, as usual, in his computer games, but for once he didn't protest when her mother told him it was time for bed.

"What's going on?" Kerry asked them.

Her mother looked at her father, then they both looked at her, grinning broadly.

"It's a surprise," her mother said.

"What is?"

Her mother looked at her father. "We're going to Florida on Saturday, Kerry," he said.

Kerry's face dropped. "Oh, no," she said, under her breath.

Her mother looked at her. "You always wanted to go to America," she said.

"Er yes," Kerry said, looking from her mother to her father and then back to her mother. She *had* always wanted go to America: she still did, but not if it meant two weeks away from Jake.

"We wanted it to be a surprise," her mother said, again.

"Yes," Kerry said dully.

She went upstairs and threw herself on her bed, cursing inwardly, wondering how she could get out of it. She didn't want to hurt her parents, but she didn't want to go away, either. A little later, the irony of it struck her – a month or so ago, she'd've loved to have gone, she really wanted to see America. Now, all she wanted to do was to see Jake.

Jake picked up the phone and dialled her number. As he waited for it to be answered, he twisted the cord into a spiral; he was gripping the handset so tightly that his fingers ached.

A man picked up the phone, her father, he supposed. He asked for her then waited a moment longer, taking a deep breath to get rid of the tremor in his voice.

"Hello?" she said.

"It's Jake."

"Hi." Her voice was a little flat.

Jake hesitated for a moment, then he plunged in, thinking that he might as well, because he'd spent so long working out what to say.

"The money from Reflex hasn't come through yet," he said, "and I'm still paying for the guitar so I'm not very rich. Actually, I'm broke. But the gig in Manchester, it went really well, and I've got another one in London this week, you know, the same place I played before? So I was wondering if you'd like to come. And the new songs, they're going pretty well, so I was thinking, if you've got time, you could maybe come round one afternoon and listen to them. I'd like you to hear them and tell me what you think. Maybe tomorrow?"

Kerry didn't reply.

Oh, no, Jake thought, I've got it all wrong, she's not interested after all.

"I mean," he said quickly, "I'd really like to take you out properly, you know, but right now it's kind of difficult because I borrowed from Dad to pay for the guitar. It won't always be like this, when the money from the gigs come through I'll be OK, but I was just thinking the other day, when I was working on the songs, that I'd really like you to be here with me. So I decided to tell you that. I know it's boring…"

"Jake," she said.

"I mean, I keep on stopping and starting, playing the same chords again and again until I've got them right, but we could have coffee and talk in-between times, and you're good at writing, maybe you could help me with the words…"

"JAKE!" she said.

"What?"

"I'd really like to come and listen to you. I really would."

"You're kidding," he gulped.

"I'm not. I—" She took a breath. "I *like* listening to you play. I like it a lot."

"You do?"

"I do. I'd really like to come round and listen to your songs. I'm glad you asked."

Relief swept over Jake like an ocean wave. "I'll pick you up tomorrow at the paper," he said. "At three. OK?"

"OK. And I'll … I'll try to come on Sunday, too."

"I'll pay for your ticket. I mean, I can afford that much. And Tony, he pays for a taxi back. We get a free meal…"

"I can pay for my own ticket," she said.

"No, you don't."

"If I can come, I will," she said.

"OK. See you tomorrow."

Kerry thought for a moment, then she went into the study, where her father was finishing some work he'd brought home with him. There was a holiday brochure open on the table – she winced when she saw scribbles on the page adding up how much it would cost.

She murmured a prayer, then she told her father that she didn't want to go on holiday at all.

He frowned.

"I was thinking," she said, "maybe Kate would like to come and stay with me."

Kate was Kerry's cousin, three years older than her.

"I mean, Dad, there's no point in taking me all that way and spending all that money if I don't want to go, is there?"

He shook his head. "What if you change your mind after we leave?"

"I won't," she said, with certainty.

He thought for a moment, then he said that she could stay, but only if her grandmother could come to stay with her.

Kerry waited nervously as he phoned her grandmother; when the old lady agreed, she whooped with glee and hugged him joyfully.

Jake met her after work the next day. Kerry felt his shyness as he took her down to the studio he'd built in the basement of his house – he kept apologizing for everything.

He settled her into the most comfortable chair, then he went back upstairs, coming back a moment later with a glass and a bottle of freshly squeezed orange juice.

"I know you like OJ," he said, "if you don't like the songs, at least, there's something you'd like."

"Jake," she said.

He put a tape on, and began to play along with it. The music was different to the songs she'd heard in the mall, it was a catchy tune played to a disco rhythm.

He played for a while, then put his guitar down and turned the tape off.

"That's good," she said.

"Yeah, but it's not what I'm supposed to be doing. That's just something that came into my head yesterday, after I'd talked to you."

She smiled. "As quickly as that?"

"It's like I said, the tunes just come to me." He picked up the guitar again, and began to play a softer tune with a haunting rhythm. It was a song about a child, being told off by his mother, not really knowing the reason why.

"I was in the supermarket one day," Jake said, when he'd finished. "There was a little boy with this woman. She was getting really hassled and she kept telling him off. He just looked at her, he didn't know what was going on."

Kerry liked it and said so.

"Thing is, these gigs Tony's getting me, I do one or two spots of about fifty minutes each. That means ten songs at least. It's a lot of material."

She nodded.

"And it's got to be all ballads, you know? Or mostly ballads. I can't do rock, at least, not hard rock."

"You do an hour at the mall."

"Yes, but I get a lot of requests. This has got to be my own stuff. Like on Sunday, it's the second time I've played the venue, so I don't want to do the same songs again."

"Why don't you play me what you're going to play then? I'll tell you if I don't like it."

Jake began to play. After a couple of numbers, he stopped. "You're bored," he said.

"No, I'm not. Actually, I'm enjoying it."

"You're kidding me."

"I'm not."

He put down the guitar and stood up and stretched, rubbing the small of his back. She sensed he wasn't going to play any more, and she was disappointed, in a way.

"Let's go for a walk," he said.

They went to the duck pond in the park, where it was quiet now that the children had all gone home.

"How many songs have you written?"

"I don't know. Hundreds. Most of them are rubbish."

"No!"

"Yes. I used to write when I was at school. The tunes are OK but the lyrics are cruddy. I've got about ten that are OK, and another ten that'll do."

"So you've got enough."

"I guess."

They sat down on one of the benches that overlooked the water.

"Thing is," he said, "even after I get the money from Reflex, I won't have much to spend. I've to pay for the guitar, and then there's college."

"So?"

He looked at her. "What I'm trying to say, I guess, is that I can't afford to take you out to the country club, or places like that. At least, not yet.

If the record sells, it'll be different, but you know there's not much chance of that."

"I can't imagine you in the country club, Jake."

He winced. "It's not my scene."

"It's not mine either. I can't stand the place."

"No? Why not?"

"It's full of these old guys in shorts with mobile phones sticking out the back pocket, and all these women with sunbed perma-tans. And you don't go to have fun, you go to have everybody else watching you look as if you're having fun. It's kind of…"

"Phony," he said, "that's what I think."

He sat back thinking for a while, and she waited, wondering what he was going to say next. He fidgeted with his nails, the ones on his right hand that were slightly longer so that he could strum his strings.

"What I'm trying to say is…"

She looked at him. "Yes, Jake?"

"Right now, I've got zip prospects and even less money, but I really like being with you and I'd really like it if we could make it a regular thing. Hell, what I'm trying to say is that I want to see more of you, Kerry. A lot more."

Kerry felt as if the world had stopped spinning, she was so dizzy that she almost swooned.

"I know," he went on, "you're probably thinking, who is this guy? I can't wine you and dine you, all I can afford is maybe a movie once a month…"

She laughed. "I'm not thinking that, not at all."

"What are you thinking, then?"

"That I really like being with you too. That I'd like to spend more time with you. That it doesn't matter about money at all, because apart from anything I'm going to be doing some work for the paper, so if you take me to a movie once a month, I'll take you for a pizza afterwards."

He stood up and picked her up and swung her around with glee, then he put her down and they stood staring into each other's eyes for an age.

The church bells began to chime, they struck seven then eight.

Jake frowned. "I'm late for the *trattoria*," he said.

They ran all the way to the High Street, laughing.

On Friday, at the mall, Corinne turned up as if nothing had happened, wearing the new jeans and T-shirt that she'd bought in New York.

Zoey shook her head, as she gayly offered to buy coffees for them all.

"Gimme a break," Corinne said. "I've said sorry and all that."

Zoey looked at Kerry, who shrugged, thinking it would be difficult to ignore Corinne for ever.

"So, what's new?" Corinne said. "I hear you split with Simon."

Zoey nodded. "It'd been coming for a while."

"You want to come to the country club tomorrow?"

"No, I'm going to henna my hair."

They listened to Jake as Corinne sat back in her chair, with a thoughtful expression on her face. Zoey nudged her as Jake finished his spot. "Come on," she said, "it's time for us to go."

Corinne didn't move. "I haven't finished my coffee yet."

Zoey looked at Kerry, shaking her head.

Kerry didn't care. She was sure how Jake felt now, sure how she felt as well.

As he walked towards her, she saw Corinne staring at him. His hair had been cut for the photo-session, he was looking terrific. His clothes were different too: he wore baggy cotton trousers and an expensive jacket, although Kerry hardly noticed that.

He put his guitar down and then sat besides Kerry.

"You're looking good," Corinne said, as her eyes swept over him.

Jake looked embarrassed. "Just some things they bought for the photo-session. I didn't have time to change."

"Looks Italian, *veree* expensive," Corinne said.

"I wouldn't know."

Kerry went and got Jake a Coke. Corinne made no move to finish her coffee, although Zoey was glaring at her.

"So, when's your record coming out?" Corinne asked him.

"Next month."

She smiled in that devilish way of hers. "My father could help you, you know. He used to be at the BBC. He knows the people on Top of the Pops. He could maybe get you on the show."

Kerry watched Jake, saw his face change. She felt a rush of rage at Corinne for doing that to him.

"I don't think so," Jake said. "They virtually only play stuff from the 'A' list, that's the main play list for Radio 1. My record won't be on it."

"You never know," Corinne said. "My father's really big in entertainment. If he put in a word for you, it'd be bound to help."

Jake shook his head. "I'd rather you didn't."

Corinne pouted. "I was only trying to help."

"Thanks, but I don't need it." He drank the Coke, then he turned to Kerry.

"Let's go."

Kerry felt Corinne's eyes drill into her back as they walked out of the mall.

14

The phone rang on Sunday, just before Kerry had to leave to go to London with Jake. Her grandmother was in the living-room, engrossed in an old movie.

Kerry picked it up, afraid that it was Jake, calling to cancel for some reason.

"Hello," Corinne said.

Kerry blinked. "I..."

"You'd better listen to what I'm going to say, Kerry."

"I'm not interested, whatever it is."

"You're not interested in Jake's career, then?"

Kerry said nothing.

"You made a fool of me," Corinne said. "I don't like being made a fool of. And I don't like being treated like dirt, either."

"Oh, no? Why d'you act like it, then?"

"Kerry, I'm warning you, I'll stop Jake dead. I'll make sure that even the pirates don't play that record of his. You better believe it, one word from my father and he's finished. And I mean dead."

"Have you ever listened to yourself, Corinne?"

"What?"

"Have you ever listened to yourself?"

"I … I don't…"

"If you did, you wouldn't say things like that," Kerry said, "because you'd know how stupid you sound."

She put the receiver down without saying goodbye, then she sat down on the stairs, shaking. She waited anxiously for a moment, but her grandmother was slightly deaf, she hadn't even heard the phone ring.

The doorbell went then, she opened it and saw Jake standing there with a smile that made her heart ache. She picked up her bag and went out, forcing herself to smile back at him.

On the train, she watched the green fields of Surrey flash by, then the jungle of the suburbs, little boxlike houses that looked all the same. Corinne's words rang in her ears – she couldn't help being afraid that she'd do something, and Jake's career was so new, so fragile that she could really hurt him.

"What's up?" Jake asked.

"Huh?"

"Kerry, you haven't said a word for ages."

"Oh," she said. "I'm just a little nervous."

"About the gig?"

"Yes," she lied.

The gig was in a restaurant in Soho, one long, thin room with a bar at the front and then tables packed together so tightly that Kerry wondered how the waiters got through.

"This is a happening place in the music business," Jake whispered.

She smiled. "How d'you tell?"

"Tony said so. He *knows*."

The walls were plastered with posters. She jumped when she saw a big picture of Jake, with *Sunday at 8* scrawled over it in a felt-tipped pen. The manager came and said hello, then led them to a table squeezed against a tiny stage.

Jake checked the tuning of his guitar.

Kerry watched as people came in and sat down. When the waitress came to take their order, she asked for iced water.

"It's on the house," the waitress said, smiling.

Kerry blushed and said iced water would be fine. She looked at Jake and saw the strain on his face: she reached over and told him that he'd be OK.

He grinned broadly. Just then a man came up and joined them.

"This is Tony, Tony Steiger, my manager," Jake said, as he reached out and shook Kerry's hand.

"So you're Kerry," he said.

"Yes," she said, wondering what Jake had told him.

Tony looked at his watch, said it was nearly time to start.

Jake picked up his guitar then stepped up to the stage, strumming a chord to check the tuning one final time.

Then he began to play, and Kerry's heart flipped. When he paused between numbers, there was a burst of applause and she was so proud that people were enjoying listening to him.

"He's good, isn't he?" Tony said, half-way through the set.

Kerry nodded, not wanting to talk.

"I mean," Tony said, "watch the audience. They're really listening to him."

Kerry looked around and saw that it was true.

"I'm hoping to get him a contract for an album, once we've got this single out of the way."

Kerry blinked and shuddered, she couldn't help it.

"Is something wrong?" he asked her.

"No," she said.

When Jake finished, the applause was louder, and it lasted for a long time. He sat down, brushing his hair back.

"You did good," Tony said; then he pointed out two DJs from Capital Radio. Jake winced, and then went to change his T-shirt, because the one he was wearing was soaked with sweat.

Kerry leaned towards Tony. "I was wondering," she said nervously, "could anyone do anything to hurt Jake's career?"

He frowned. "How d'you mean?"

Kerry shrugged, tried to be nonchalant. "You know, some of the people at home, they're really jealous of him."

Tony nodded. "I'm not surprised."

"I was just worried that they might *do* something..."

"What could they do? Thing is, Kerry, virtually anything they do'll make it better. If they're bad-mouthing him, it'll only help."

"How?"

Tony sat back. "That old adage about all publicity being good publicity. Half, no, ninety per cent of the stuff you read in the tabloids is gossip, not fact. It's rubbish, most of it. But it excites peoples' interest, so they buy the records."

Kerry nodded.

"If people in Alton talk, as they're more or less bound to, it'll only make people buy Jake's record. So long as the talk doesn't hurt you or him, there's no problem. The way the market is, there's zillions of records and anything that draws people's attention to his record, that makes them listen to it, is good. It's a great record, remember. If people listen to it, they'll buy it.

"So don't worry, Kerry."

She turned round, saw Jake coming back with a fresh T-shirt on.

Tony Steiger patted her head. "Trust me," he said. "It's not as if he's upset a DJ or a big producer or anything like that."

Kerry blinked.

Tony ordered steak fajitas all around, then he asked Jake if he'd do another spot afterwards.

"OK, so long as it's OK with Kerry," he said.

Kerry struggled to smile. "It's fine."

In the car going back to Alton, he reached out and grasped her hand. Kerry, deep in torment about Corinne's threats, jumped.

"What is it?" he asked her.

"Er ... nothing, Jake."

He glanced at the driver. "You're really quiet. Are you OK?"

"That steak fajita, it was a bit spicy."

"Oh. What did you think of the gig?"

"It was good, Jake. *You* were good."

When the car stopped outside her house, he got out too. Kerry saw the living-room lights still on; her grandmother was still up, waiting for her.

"I ... I'd ask you in for a coffee, but Gran's there."

He nodded. "Thanks for coming, anyway."

"Thanks for taking me, Jake. It was great."

"How about tomorrow? D'you want to come round and help me work on some lyrics?"

"I ... er, I can't, Jake. Not tomorrow."

He gazed at her for a moment, then he leaned towards her and kissed her softly on the forehead.

"Soon, then?"

"Yes, Jake. I'll see you soon."

Kerry raced upstairs and threw herself on to her bed, where she punched her pillow in anger. She only stopped when she heard her grandmother's soft footsteps on the stairs; a moment later, the old lady opened her bedroom door, holding a cup of cocoa.

When Kerry finished telling Zoey all about it, Zoey rubbed her eyes hard, then she rested her chin in her hands.

"Jeez," she said, "I don't know."

"I don't know either," Kerry said.

"Corinne's father *is* a big producer. And he worships the ground she walks on."

"Thing is, I don't know him. I've met him a couple of times, and he seemed OK. He didn't seem mean, or anything. Like he'd have to be mean, to do something like that to Jake."

"I've known him for years," Zoey said. "He's got this big blind spot where Corinne's concerned. I don't *think* he'd do anything, but I don't know."

"Yeah. I keep on telling myself Corinne's just making empty threats, but I can't help being afraid for Jake. Y'see, it's *my* fault. If I hadn't liked Jake, Corinne wouldn't've bothered with him."

Zoey leaned over and touched her hand. "It's not your fault," she said.

Kerry winced.

"I could talk to Corinne," Zoey said.

"No!"

"I could maybe try to make her see sense."

"The way she is, she's so mad, you might make her worse."

Zoey sighed. "So what are you going to do?"

Kerry shook her head. "I don't know."

The note was lying on the hall table beside the phone when she got in: *Jake called, please call him back.*

Kerry went into the kitchen to make coffee. Her grandmother was making cup-cakes.

"Who's Jake?" she asked her.

"Just a friend."

She stirred milk into her coffee, then went to return the call.

Jake's voice was light and happy. "I've got the release date for the record," he said, "it'll be out on the second Friday of September."

Kerry gasped.

"I thought you'd like to know," he said, carefully. "You said you wanted to write about it."

"I do," she said.

"So, what're you doing?"

Kerry opened her mouth to say "nothing", then she thought again. "I ... um, Gran's here, you know, she wants to go shopping, she wants to go up to London to see the sights."

"You sound kind of tied up," Jake said.

"Well, just for a few days. I don't like to leave her alone too much."

"I'll see you around then."

"Yes."

"OK," he said.

Kerry put the phone down, her heart aching. She went upstairs to her room and sat down at her desk to think.

Corinne's face flashed before her, her sly smile and her mannerisms, the way she gayly ran up vast bills on her father's credit card without a second thought.

Kerry tried to rationalize, to tell herself that no man in his position would wilfully destroy a young musician's career just on his daughter's say-so, but all her reasoning didn't work, she was still terrified.

She kept on thinking that Corinne might spin some tale about Jake: she might tell her father he'd been nasty to her or, much worse, that he'd made a move on her and had been aggressive about it, the kind of thing that would make any father furious.

She even found herself wishing that she'd never come to Alton, she'd never met Jake; if she'd stayed in Cumbria, none of this would have happened, his record would be on its way without the dark cloud of Corinne's fury hanging over it.

The day passed somehow. She lay in bed that night, awake, unable to sleep or even rest because of the worry.

The idea came in the wee small hours long after midnight, when even the church clock was silent and the rest of Alton was asleep. Corinne had told her once that her father worked out religiously, every morning, in the gym at the country club. If Kerry went there and met him, he'd think it was an accident, and she'd have a chance to talk to him discreetly, to find out what Corinne had done, if anything.

She set her alarm for 6.30, then she turned over and tried to sleep.

When the alarm went off, she jumped up and dressed quickly in shorts and her school tracksuit; the Smiths weren't members of the country club but, if she looked the part, maybe she'd manage to slip in.

When she reached the country club, though, Corinne's father's car wasn't in the car park. She ran round the perimeter a couple of times, but it didn't appear.

Finally, shivering in the morning chill, she asked the attendant if Mr Ford was there.

He looked her up and down. "He's been and gone, love. Comes at six, when we open. Away at half past. You an actress or something?"

"No. I'm … I'm a friend of his daughter's."

"She won't be in till later, if you want to be signed in."

Kerry turned to leave, furious with herself.

Jake was sitting in a marketing meeting at the record company. They were talking about how they were going to promote the single.

The marketing manager and the publicist had gone through a long list of DJs, allocating someone to phone each one of them to check that they'd received the single and to try and persuade them to listen to it.

Tim Sloan was there, and so was Tony Steiger. Each of them had made a list of people they'd call as well.

Jake felt bad, because he could do little himself. He didn't know any DJs, or anyone who was important in the music business – the only contact he had was with Corinne's father, and he didn't want to mention that because he was sure that there were strings attached.

He felt even worse because of Kerry; something had happened to her. It had been going so well, he thought, and then, all of sudden, she'd gone all cool on him. That night they'd gone to the gig, she'd been all quiet and then, later, she'd seemed not to want to see him again. When he'd phoned her the next day, she had phoned back, but she'd been vague, as if she had better things to do with her time than spend it with him.

He felt hurt deep inside, he liked her so much, had been so sure that she liked him.

"Jake!" Tim said, loudly.

He looked up and saw them all looking at him.

"Er, I'm sorry," he said.

"Kit was asking you about the lyrics," Tim said. "And the title. How come you called it *Kerry's Song*?"

Kit Carmichael was the publicist; she was bright and young and, right now, she was beaming at him.

"Uh," Jake said, feeling a dull ache in his stomach as he remembered those early days in the mall, when he'd watched her from a distance and fallen in love with her.

"Kerry's a girl," he said, slowly. "She was watching me in the mall one day, and I liked the way that she smiled. So I wrote the song about her."

He blushed deeply. Kerry didn't know about the title yet, he'd meant it to be a surprise, but the way she'd been the last few days, he wasn't sure if she even cared or not.

"And where is she now?" Kit asked him.

Jake shifted in his seat. "In Alton, I s'pose."

"Are the two of you going out?"

"I ... er, not really."

Tony looked sharply at him.

"I've met Kerry, haven't I?" Tim Sloan said. "She's the reporter? With long brown hair and brown eyes?"

Jake nodded.

Tim Sloan looked at Kit Carmichael. "She's got that look about her. You know, pretty but vulnerable? She'd photograph well."

Jake frowned.

"Sounds good," Kit said, looking at Jake. "What I mean is, we get a couple of good shots of Kerry and give it to one of the papers. You know, the story behind the song. It's the kind of thing they love."

"Uh," Jake said. He was thinking, maybe Kerry wouldn't like to be used like that. Maybe she'd think he was interested in her just because of the record. The way she'd been recently, she might not be interested at all.

"So, what d'you say, Jake? Can I put it together?"

He faced the publicist. "No," he said. "At least, not yet. Not till I've talked to her."

Tim Sloan frowned. "It's a good story, Jake. It could make all the difference."

"No," Jake said, again.

"But…"

Tony cut in. "You heard what he said."

When the meeting broke up, he took Jake aside. "Look," he said, "I'm not going to force you, I can't, but will you at least talk to Kerry, ask her about it?"

Jake said nothing.

"There's a lot riding on this single," Tony said.

"I'm not going to use Kerry like that!" Jake said, sharply.

Tony sighed. "It's not like that. I don't know her that well, but she seemed to really want to help you. Why not give her the chance?"

"I … I'll think about it," Jake said.

On the train home, he thought, and the more he thought, the more he became afraid that, if he asked Kerry, she would think he was using her.

Whatever he did, Jake wasn't going to do that.

On Wednesday morning, Kerry was waiting outside the country club at a quarter to six. In her pocket, she'd a ticket she'd bought the previous day; it had cost a lot of money, but it was the only way to get in.

When the doors opened, she slipped inside and watched from the window as Mr Ford drove in. He didn't even notice her as he headed straight for the pool, where he did twenty lengths.

Kerry watched him, frustrated; he was intent on his exercise.

He got out of the pool and headed for the changing-room. Kerry glanced at the clock, and prayed that he wasn't going to leave just yet. He re-emerged a minute later and headed for the weight machines in the gym, where he began to pump iron.

Kerry took the machine besides him.

"Hi," she said.

He said hello automatically, then he stopped pumping iron and looked at her.

"It's Kerry, isn't it? What are you doing here so early?"

Kerry took a deep breath, and said that she wanted to talk to him.

His brow furrowed, he turned the rep counter off and turned to face her. "What is it? It's not Corinne, is it?"

"Not exactly," she said, quickly. "It's just that

Corinne and I ... there's this boy called Jake, he sings at the mall..."

"Yes. I saw your story in the *Gazette*."

"Y'see, Jake's got a single coming out soon, and I was thinking, I mean, you being a producer..."

The furrows on his brow deepened. "I can't do anything for him, if that's what you mean."

"It's not that," Kerry said. "It's just, you know, Jake and I, we started seeing each other, and Corinne, well, she sort of got annoyed about it, I don't know why, but she got pretty mad and she said, one word from you and you could wreck Jake's career... I mean, there wasn't a row or anything, he didn't do anything to her, he hardly even knows her, but I was really worried about it, so I thought I'd talk to you and explain. Nothing happened except Corinne got angry and we fell out, and it would be really terrible if Jake's career was ruined because of that..."

Corinne's father sighed. "Let me get this straight. You and Corinne, you both liked the same boy, and he ends up with you, so Corinne got hurt..."

"Jake didn't hurt her," Kerry said quickly. "Corinne didn't even like him at first, it was only after he got the contract. She said you could get him Top of the Pops but he said he'd rather not. You see, he doesn't want anyone to pull strings for him. Corinne got mad then. She phoned me and made all sorts of threats."

"Ah," he got off the machine, glancing at his watch.

Kerry blinked, sure she'd said the wrong thing.

"I was just afraid..." she mumbled.

"Corinne did say something about this Jake, I can't remember what," he said. "Thing is, I produce game shows mostly, I've nothing to do with the music business 'cept for booking the odd act."

"Oh," Kerry said.

"And I wouldn't do anything to the guy, not unless he'd done something really terrible to Corinne, and if he'd done that, I'd call the police."

"Oh," Kerry said again. "I just thought I'd talk to you, I was so worried, you see."

"There's no need to be worried on my account," he said. "As for Corinne, well, I'm sorry that the two of you've fallen out, I just hope you make it up, that's all."

Kerry smiled thinly. "Yes," she said, "thanks."

When she got home, she took the little tape recorder out of the pocket of her tracksuit, where she'd hidden it, then she took the tape out and threw it away.

She'd felt terrible about using it, but she felt she had to, because if Corinne's father *had* threatened Jake, then at least she could prove it and then, if she'd given the tape to Tony Steiger, maybe he could have done something about it.

Later that day, Kerry began to draft a story about the record being released; she wanted to use it for her first column. Half-way through writing it, she remembered that *The Girl With The Smile In Her Eyes* was the song's working title, she didn't know the final one. She picked up the phone to call

Jake, then she decided to call the record company instead.

"Hello," she said, nervously. "This is Kerry Smith. I'm calling about—"

"Are you *the* Kerry?" the woman who answered the phone said.

"I ... I don't know..."

"Jake's friend Kerry? The one he wrote the song about?"

"I..."

"It's called *Kerry's Song*, Kerry. Jake wrote it about a girl he met in the mall..."

A wave of dizziness swept over Kerry. "I ... I didn't know that."

"Kerry, am I glad to talk to you, you see..."

A few minutes later, Kerry put the phone down, then she ran round to Jake's. His sister let her into the house, and then opened the door to the basement, yelling to Jake that Kerry was on her way.

He was working on a song, he put down the guitar and looked at her.

"Why didn't you tell me, Jake?"

"Tell you what? D'you mean *Kerry's Song*?"

Kerry shook her head, although that was part of it. "I mean about the story, the story about us."

"You phoned the record company," he said flatly.

"I had to, to check the story I was doing. They told me. They said it could make the record."

Jake got up and turned the amplifier off, then he unplugged the leads and switched off the tape recorder, and put his guitar into its case.

"Come on," he said, "we've got a lot of talking to do."

172

*   *   *

They walked down to the river and then along the bank until they were out of the town. Although the day was warm, there was a chill in the air that heralded the end of the summer.

What a summer it had been, Kerry thought, remembering the doubts and uncertainties that she had felt about Jake and her future.

"You should've told me that you'd called it *Kerry's Song*," she said.

Jake smiled. "I was going to. But you know how I'm shy, and it never felt that the time was right. And then, the other day, I thought you'd gone off me."

"Never," she said, then she told him all about Corinne's threats, how worried she'd been and how she'd gone to talk to Corinne's father.

He put his arm around her, and she felt a shiver run right down her spine.

"You should've told me."

"Jake, I *couldn't*. I had to try to sort it out myself."

"I'm glad you did. But, next time, tell me, huh?"

"OK," she said. "What are we going to do about the story?"

"Well," he said, "I thought about it a lot, and I decided I don't want to do it."

She stopped walking and turned to face him.

"Why not? The PR woman said it would be really good for the record."

"Yes, but it's not just the record, it's about us, Kerry. It's about you and me. I don't want to see us splattered all over the papers. It's my first record, and I'd like to see if I can make it on the strength of my music, not just record company hype. I'd feel better that way."

Jake gazed at her for a moment, then he gathered her into his arms and kissed her, gently at first and then with confidence. His tongue strayed around her lips, and then gently parted them; Kerry felt that she would die with happiness, she didn't want him to stop kissing her, ever.

They kissed for a long time, until he was out of breath and she was dizzy.

Afterwards, he held her tightly.

"You know," she said, "I've just realized, the story might come out anyway."

"How come?"

"Well, the first two stories I did about you had my byline, Kerry Smith, and this one will have, too. It doesn't take a genius to put two and two together."

"No," Jake said, "I suppose not."

EPILOGUE

When the record was released, two weeks later, Jake took Kerry to the *trattoria* to celebrate. She was wearing the leather jacket he'd bought her; the present had been a surprise, he'd bought it because he'd seen her looking at it in the mall. "Just because you're you," he'd said.

Mario made a terrible fuss of them, putting them at the best table and then insisting on giving them a glass of champagne each on the house.

Kerry was utterly thrilled; it was her birthday next week, and, as she sat with Jake, she thought that she could not have had a better present; even the leather jacket did not compare to just being with him.

They were together now; she adored being with Jake and, as she looked at him, she knew he felt the same way about being with her.

She didn't notice the music playing in the background, but Jake, ever the musician, did.

"Hey, Mario," he said, when Mario brought their starters of mozzarella and tomato salad, "how come you're playing Radio 1?"

"Er, tape is bust," Mario said, before he disappeared in the direction of the kitchen.

Kerry smiled at Jake. "What's the matter?"

"It gives me the jitters, listening to Radio 1," he said. "I mean, today's the first day they can play my record. But they won't, of course. It's just I'd rather not listen to them not playing it."

Kerry laughed. "Don't be so negative," she said. "Zoey heard it on Atlantic 252. If they're playing it, Radio 1 might."

"Maybe," he said. "But I daren't hope. You know the numbers, each week they play only fifty or sixty records. I haven't got much of a chance."

"I don't know," Kerry said. She was feeling good about the future.

The record ended, and the DJ began to announce the next one. Jake held out his hands to show Kerry that they were shaking. She reached over and clasped them in hers.

"Don't worry," she said.

Although the salad was delicious, she noticed that Jake stopped eating when the record came to an end. He went pale as the DJ began to speak again.

Kerry tried to ignore the DJ and concentrate on Jake.

"Great mozzarella," she said, thinking that, if the record was going to get airplay, Jake would hear it anyway without listening as if the DJ was a judge about to hand down a death sentence.

"And the dressing's dreamy."

Suddenly Jake's eyes widened.

Kerry began to listen too, hardly daring to hope.

"...ichaels," the DJ was saying. "It's a new release on Reflex Records, and I think it's going to go places. So, here's *Kerry's Song*, and remember, you heard it first on Radio 1."

Kerry screamed as the first bars of *Kerry's Song* began to play.

Jake jumped out of his chair and then picked her up, spinning her round and round until Kerry felt dizzy and had to ask him to put her down.

The song was still playing. Jake whooped with glee and then Mario caught him in a bear-hug and the pair of them sang along with the tune like star-struck fans.

Tears were steaming down Kerry's cheeks when the song finished.

"*Kerry's Song*, by Jake Michaels," the DJ said. "I've a feeling that record is going to be played at the end of a lot of Christmas parties. A lot of other parties, come to that. It's the best love song I've heard for years. And now..."

Jake couldn't speak for a moment. Mario opened another bottle of champagne and he gave a glass to everyone in the restaurant. When they realized who Jake was, everyone clapped, and Jake shyly took a bow. He'd given Mario an advance copy of the single, which Mario had made him sign and then stuck up on the wall.

When the fuss had died down, Mario joined them.

"How did you know?" Jake asked him.

"I didn't *know*, but my sister's 'usband, 'is brother's daughter ees secretary at BBC. I ask 'er. She say, she don't know, *but*, the DJ on Saturday night likes it and 'ee *might* play eet. So I put radio on, and 'ope."

Jake laughed. Kerry was so happy that she hugged Mario to thank him.

His face went bright red and he left to go back to the kitchen, telling them first to enjoy their meal.

The meal was perfect, Kerry thought, as she finished her *tiramisu* ice-cream. Everything was perfect, most of all, being with Jake.

"Told you you'd make it," she said.

He shrugged. "I never thought I'd feel this way, but it doesn't matter so much now, my record making it, I mean."

She frowned. "No?"

"No," he said, "what really matters is, I've made it with you."

P⦁INT CRiME

If you like Point Horror, you'll love Point Crime!

Look out for the spine-jangling new crime series from Malcolm Rose:

LAWLESS &
TILLEY

LAWLESS: Brett. Detective Inspector with a lot to prove. Biochemical background. Hot on analysis but prone to wild theories. *Dangerous.*

TILLEY: Clare. Detective Sergeant with her feet on the ground. Tough and intuitive. Completely sane. *She needs to be.*

THE CASE: 1. *The Secrets of the Dead*
Four bodies have been found in the Peak District. They're rotting fast and vital evidence needs to be taken from the corpses. You need a strong stomach to work in Forensics...

THE CASE: 2. *Deep Waters*
Colin Games has died after a bizarre illness. A post-mortem reveals no obvious cause of death, but the pathologist isn't happy. Enlarged liver, anaemia, heart irregularities – it all points to *poison*...

Join **Lawless & Tilley** as they pick over the clues. But be warned: it's no job for the fainthearted.

Point Horror

Are you hooked on horror? Thrilled by fear? Then these are the books for you. A powerful series of horror fiction designed to keep you quaking in your shoes.

Point Horror

Point Horror

Dare you read

NIGHTMARE HALL

Where college is a
scream!

High on a hill overlooking Salem University
hidden in shadows and shrouded in
mystery, sits Nightingale Hall.

Nightmare Hall, the students call it.
Because that's where the terror began...

Don't miss these spine-tingling thrillers: